CYNTHIA HICKEY

A GOOD PARTY CAN KILL YOU

A Nosy Neighbor Mystery
Book 7

By Cynthia Hickey

Copyright © 2015 **Written by: Cynthia Hickey**
Published by: Winged Publications
Cover Design: Cynthia Hickey

This book is a work of fiction. Names, characters, places, and incidents are the product of the author's imagination and are used fictitiously. Any resemblance to actual events, locales, or persons, living or dead, is coincidental.

No part of this book may be copied or distributed without the author's consent.

-
- **ISBN-13:** 978-1-0879-8090-4

To God and my family who give me the
encouragement to write..

ACKNOWLEDGMENTS

Thank you to my readers who are always eagerly awaiting the next mystery..

1

"That's Matt's ex!" Maryann pointed at a voluptuous brunette heading into a voodoo store.

The woman glanced our way, scowled, and ducked out of sight.

I couldn't help but compare myself to the gorgeous woman. I, Stormi Nelson, was more lean lines than soft curves. Not to mention the woman looked better in shorts and a tank top than I ever would, even in formal wear.

I grabbed my best friend's arm. "Come on. We don't have time to worry about her." Although, I wouldn't have minded a bit of spying on the woman who had been Matt's first. "We still have things to buy for the party tonight." Preparations for my bachelorette party were going to kill me.

With my wedding a month away, my sister, Angela had broached the wonderful idea of a week long bachelorette party in New Orleans. Of course, all those invited gave an excited, "Yay!" Except me. I would have preferred a quiet night at home with popcorn and a chick flick.

After a night of sightseeing and scaring ourselves silly in an ancient graveyard, I still needed to purchase the matching tee shirts I'd ordered for the last hoorah. We were dining and partying on the Mississippi river with a dinner cruise on our last night before heading home. I couldn't wait to see Matt again.

"It wouldn't hurt to see what she's up to in New Orleans. She's a world traveling photographer, you know." Maryann craned her neck as I pulled her into a novelty shop. "We've always had very interesting conversations."

"I do not want to talk about Matt to his ex-girlfriend. Not at my bachelorette."

I approached the sales counter. "One tee shirt for the bride and three for bridesmaids. I received a call this morning that they were ready."

"Right here." The clerk, a bubbly teen, chomped her gum and handed me a bright yellow bag. "Congratulations on your wedding. How exciting!"

"How did you know she was the bride?" Maryann leaned against the counter.

"I…guessed?" The clerk shrugged. "Does it matter?"

"No, but someday, it'll be me." She grabbed the bag from my hand, swung it over her shoulder, and sashayed out the door.

I exchanged an amused look with the clerk and followed my maid-of-honor. "What was that about?"

"I want to get married." She pouted and headed down the sidewalk. "I'm going to buy a love potion and dump it in Michael's coffee."

"He isn't worth having if you have to use trickery." Oh, no. My friend was opening the door to the very shop Matt's old girlfriend had gone into. Maybe she had left. I glanced around the street. No such luck.

"Why, hello, Maryann." A voice so smooth it could melt ice drifted through the open door. "What brings you to New Orleans?"

"I'm the maid-of-honor in Matt's wedding. This is Stormi Nelson, bride-to-be and best-selling author." She grabbed my arm and swung me around to face who could only be my new nemesis. I seriously doubted whether we would be friends.

"I'm Rachel Gable, old news." She thrust out a manicured hand and gave a smile that didn't quite meet her eyes. "I'd heard rumors about Matthew getting married, but I never thought I'd see the day."

"Why not?" I pulled my hand free.

"He's more the wandering type. Like me. Ta ta, girls. See you on the flipside." She moseyed down the sidewalk with a hip sway that would break a lesser woman's back.

Maryann cocked her head. "Hmmm, I always thought of her as being nicer. Oh, well. Come on."

I followed her into the dim recesses of a shop full of beads, crystals, and...were those dead things? Gross. Still, I'd never been inside a voodoo shop and I took research for my novels where I could find it. I picked up a pink stopper bottle from the shelf. "Seriously? Love Potion number 9? Isn't that a song?"

"Give me that." Maryann snatched it from me. "That's what I'm looking for." She glanced at the price tag. "Fifteen dollars well spent...if it works."

I rolled my eyes and continued around the shop amazed at the variety of dolls and skull jewelry. This was the place to be if you believed in such nonsense or was a teenager lost in the world of Goth makeup and accessories.

A garnet necklace caught my eye. The sign said it guaranteed your man would love you forever as long as you wore the necklace. I chuckled and left it on the shelf. I was already succumbing to the traditions of something old, something new, something borrowed, and something blue. I had no reason to add dark magic, not when my faith followed the light.

"I'm ready." Maryann grinned, dropped the bottle into the bag with the tee shirts, and sailed toward the door. "We have two hours to catch our dinner cruise."

Outside, I blinked against the late afternoon sun glinting off the reflective mirror of a hot dog stand. A woman on the opposite side of the street waved.

"Mom?" What in the world? Whose mother came to their daughter's bachelorette shindig?

"In the flesh! The others said it wouldn't matter if I tagged along, so I caught a flight in this morning."

"I don't have a tee shirt for you to wear."

"That's okay, I had one made." She pulled a shirt in the same shade as ours out of her purse. This one said in bright white letters, "Mother of the Bride." As if it couldn't get any worse, she handed me a little white veil with crystals along the headband and fabric that stuck up like a rooster's feathers. She tucked her arm in mine. "We're going to have so much fun."

A GOOD PARTY CAN KILL YOU

~

Despite trying to leave the veil behind, I led my group onboard the Steamboat Natchez with me looking like a pink chicken while the others clacked behind me. Spotting a bottle of champagne on our table, my spirits brightened immediately. Normally, I stuck to sparkling cider, but tonight, I was having a glass of champagne to celebrate.

We sat at the round table covered with a white tablecloth and raised our glasses for the server to fill them. Looking at the faces of everyone I loved, I didn't care if we looked tacky or were a little loud. I was going to have a blast.

"Whoa." I shook my head as the waiter started to fill Cherokee's glass. "She's only eighteen."

"I'll be back with something non-alcoholic," he said.

"Oh, Aunt Stormi. One glass wouldn't hurt me." My niece, who happened to be too beautiful for words and, already having lived more in her short life than most people lived in fifty years, crossed her arms.

"Maybe not, but jail would definitely hurt us all, and I'd be late to my wedding." I gave her a wink and took a sip. I grimaced. Not my favorite, but I wasn't going to be a fuddy-duddy, not tonight. Especially with my sister, Angela, narrowing her eyes at me over her glass.

"I think my daughter can have a glass," she said.

"Oops. Sorry. Too late." I grinned. Somebody needed to act like a parent. Angela and I had always suffered from sibling rivalry from the moment I was born and took over the house. Not to mention I'd had to loan her money on several occasions, and she now lived in my renovated attic. It was all a bitter pill for her to have to swallow.

Once our drinks were filled, our server set a house salad in front of us. "Served with our cane sugar dressing," he said. "The meal ordered for you tonight is our Filet Gumbo, Pilot House Potatoes, Creole Creamed Spinach, and for dessert…Natchez Bread Pudding. Enjoy!"

It all sounded wonderful. I dug into my salad, closing my eyes in sheer pleasure at the sweet tang of the dressing.

"Good evening."

I opened my eyes to the sight of Rachel in a clingy maxi dress and lacy shrug smiling down at us. "It seems as if I've crashed a bachelorette party."

"It's only crashing if we let you sit down, dear," Mom said.

I hid my grin behind my napkin. "Nice to see you again, Rachel."

"Unexpected, I'm sure." She glanced over her shoulder. "My dinner date and I always take the dinner cruise when I'm in town. I thought it rude if I didn't stop by and say hello." She stepped close to my chair and placed a hand on my shoulder. "Congratulations, again." With another cool smile, she turned and returned to her table.

"What an odd girl." Mom snapped her napkin across her lap. "She has a lot of nerve approaching us, considering who she is."

My eyes widened. "You know her?"

"She's a famous photographer, dear, and was once engaged to Matthew."

I glared at Maryann. She'd left out the

bit of information that they had actually been engaged.

She mouthed "sorry" and shoved a forkful of salad into her mouth.

"Things aren't as rosy in Stormi's world as they usually are." Angela grinned and refilled her champagne glass.

Great. I'd have to deal with a tipsy sister at my bachelorette party.

By the time we finished our delicious and very filling meal, I wished I'd worn elastic waist pants. "Let's take a walk around deck. I'm stuffed. Mom, you might want to hold Angela's hand."

My sister said a very naughty word and pushed back from the table. When she teetered on her stiletto heels, she clutched Mom's arm.

Cherokee rolled her eyes and walked away, most likely to pretend she didn't know her mother.

I followed my friends and family and took a deep breath of Mississippi river air. Nothing like the smell of water and mud to ground a person.

"Look." Maryann pointed to the opposite end of the deck. "It looks as if

Rachel is arguing with her date. I wish I could see more than just the back of his head."

"Why? You probably don't know him."

"But, what if I do?"

Good point, I guess, although I couldn't figure out why it mattered. "Let's ditch the others and mosey that way."

"It won't matter." Rachel flipped her hair. "I'll get him back. It's only a matter of time. Have you seen her? Ugh."

She couldn't possibly be talking about me and Matt, could she? Oh, I'd like to wring her—"

Maryann yanked me into an alcove. "You don't want her to see you!"

I guess I was approaching her at a rather rapid rate. "It sounds like she plans on going after Matt."

"He loves you. She doesn't stand a chance." She peered around the corner. "They're gone. Come on."

"I really don't want to spy or do any investigating on my bachelorette weekend." I turned back to where Mom and the others leaned on the railing.

"We aren't. I just want to know if she's actually going to try and break you and my brother apart. You don't want to be blindsided, do you?"

"You're contradicting yourself, Maryann. Either I have nothing to worry about, or I do."

"We're just playing it safe. Stop." She motioned to where Rachel stood a few feet away.

"I told you not to worry about it. I'll have him eating out of my hand in a week."

My gaze locked on Maryann's wide one. This did not sound good at all.

2

While I'd had a very good time in New Orleans, it was always nice to get home. Before unpacking, I took a couple of ibuprofen for a killer headache knocking on my skull, then curled up on the front porch swing and gave my hunky fiancé a call.

"I'm home," I said the moment he answered.

"Already on my way. I was watching for you."

I stood and spotted him coming down the sidewalk. I turned off my phone and jumped off the porch to run toward him.

He grabbed me in his arms and swung

me around before planting a heated kiss on my lips. "Did you have a good time?"

"Yep. I also had the displeasure of meeting your ex, Rachel." I spotted Ethel Rogers and Mrs. Olson glaring at us from their front lawns. Oh, well. The neighbors should be used to me kissing Matt in broad daylight by now.

"Maryann told me. I'm sorry about that. Do you feel all right?"

"I've had a bad headache since yesterday. It'll pass, eventually." I led him to the swing. "When was the last time you saw or spoke with her?"

"Over a year ago. Why?" He sat and pulled me onto his lap.

"I overheard her talking with someone and it sounded suspiciously as if she were plotting to break us up."

He tweaked my nose. "Impossible to do. Your new private investigator mind is working overtime."

"I hope so." I rested my head on his shoulder. "Can you stay for dinner?"

"No, I'm leaving soon for a job."

"What? I just got home." I straightened.

"I'm sorry."

Sighing, I stood. "I know. How long will you be gone?"

"No more than a week, I don't think. We should be able to crack the case pretty quickly."

I hated that he worked dangerous undercover work, but I couldn't blame him. Since my first accidental mystery a little over a year ago, I'd gotten hooked on not only outsmarting the crook, but the dollars writing the true crime mysteries brought in. Yes, I could relate to the rush he felt when closing a case. I leaned down and kissed him. "I love you. Be careful and call as often as you can."

"I will." He stood and pulled me back into his arms. "I love you, too, Stormi. Don't worry about Rachel. I doubt you'll ever see her again."

After a kiss that left me weak in the knees, he bounded down the steps, tossed me a wave, and headed to his house.

With a heavy sigh I trudged to my bedroom to unpack. I unzipped my case and tossed everything on the bed. While I might pack carefully for vacation, I threw the dirty clothes back in the suitcase in any way they would fit. They were only going in the washing machine.

I rubbed the area between my eyes and plopped on the bed. What was up with this headache? I wasn't prone to them. Could I be having a reaction to something I'd eaten?

I headed to the restroom for a cool washrag, then lay on the bed with the wet rag over my eyes. Now, I could completely empathize with people who suffered from migraines.

"Do you need help unpacking?"

I lifted the rag to see Mom peering down at me.

"What's wrong?"

"Head hurts."

She nodded. "I'll throw your dirty things in the wash for you. I've started a load." She gathered an armful.

Something fell from the pile of laundry with a muffled thud. "What a creepy souvenir. Why'd you buy this?" Mom held up a rag doll with red yarn for hair. Sticking out of its head were three hat pins.

I sat up. "I didn't buy that. Maybe Angela stuck it in there because her suitcase was too full."

"I'll ask her." Mom tossed the doll on the bed.

Ivory and Ebony, my elusive cats, charged from under the bed and pounced after the horrid thing. I smiled, despite my headache. I'd missed my kitties. Since I'd gotten Sadie, my giant Irish Wolfhound, the cats tended to avoid me. But, Sadie was outside doing her business, and the cats decided to play.

Angela stomped into my room. "I didn't stick anything in your…that's disgusting." She pointed at the doll. "Why would you buy that?"

"I didn't." I tossed the rag on the nightstand and grabbed the doll away from the cats. It really was hideous with sewn Xs for eyes, yarn hair, and a shapeless body.

"I know what that is." Angela's eyes widened. "That's a voodoo doll. See the pins? The doll is supposed to represent you. Those pins cause pain on your body wherever they are on the doll."

"That explains the headache," Mom added, coming back into the room.

"I don't believe in that stuff and neither should you two." I yanked the pins from the doll's head and laid them on the nightstand.

"Is your headache gone?" Mom asked.

Surprisingly, it was ebbing. "It has nothing to do with superstition. The real question is...how did it get into my suitcase?" If none of us put it there, it would have had to have been one of the hotel staff. But, why? Were they paid to put it there? This might be one mystery I never solved. I wasn't sure I wanted to. "Throw it away."

"Now that the pins are out, Sadie would probably like it." Mom picked it up by a strand of red yarn hair.

"That's fine. You can toss it on her bed. You're right. The animals will enjoy it." I swung my legs over the bed. My phone beeped, alerting me to a text message. It was from Dakota. **Come to my work. Don't tell anyone. Come alone. 911.**

Come quick.

Rather cryptic. "I'm heading out for coffee. Anyone want anything?"

"I'll come with you," Mom said. "I need to check in at the bakery."

Angela shook her head.

Great. I'd drop Mom off, then check on Dakota. Of course, his text did seem rather urgent. "I'm leaving now, Mom. If you aren't ready, you'll have to drive yourself."

"Wow. I've never known anyone in such a hurry for coffee in the middle of the day. Especially, someone who was dying from a headache mere seconds ago. Go without me. I'll probably be at the bakery longer than you want to hang around anyway."

"Thanks." I bounded down the stairs, grabbed my purse, and set off toward Gadgets and More, What Every Spy Needs.

The store was dark. The front door locked. I cupped my hands and peered through the front window. What was my nephew up to now?

Digging my phone from my pocket, I

sent him a text. **Door is locked. Where are you?**

Come to back door. Don't let anyone see you.

Since making him an unofficial partner in my PI business, Dakota tended to be dramatic in everyday things. Still, it wasn't like him to be this secretive.

With a glance up and down the street and, not seeing anyone, I ducked into the alley and counted doors until I reached the fifth one. The door swung open at my touch.

"Hello?"

"Back here. Close the door."

I did as instructed and made my way through the dimly lit room to a supply closet. Dakota knelt next to a computer monitor set on the floor.

"What's with all the cloak and dagger?"

"You need to see this." He pressed a button and the screen came to life.

"Where's Mr. Dixon?" It bothered me that the store was closed when it should be open and that Dakota sat in the dark by himself. My gut told me something was seriously wrong.

"I don't know. After being here for over an hour by myself, I found this video. I think it's a live stream of his house."

That got my attention. I squatted next to my nephew as the camera panned through a living room, a bedroom, and into a kitchen.

"The camera hops from room to room. I'm trying to find out whether I can rewind the tape or not. You'll see why in a minute."

I gasped. Mr. Dixon, a knife sticking out of his back, lay between the kitchen sink and the island. A pool of dark liquid spread from underneath him. "Have you called the police?"

He glanced at me. "You think this is all real?"

"Why wouldn't it be?"

"Last year, I found a similar tape on Halloween. It was a prank. But, this one is much better done."

I bit my lower lip. "Let's go to his house and check it out. I'm calling Wayne to meet us there." If it was a joke, it was a sick one.

"Why not Matt?"

"Gone on assignment." I missed him already. "Come on. I'll drive."

While we locked the back door, then made our way to my car, I dialed Wayne, Matt's partner, and left a message for him to meet us at Mr. Dixon's house. I didn't have an address, since Dakota knew the way, but the police department would find it easily enough.

Mr. Dixon lived in an upscale area of newly built homes. I preferred the character of my neighborhood full of Victorian fixer uppers being restored to their former glory. Still, the money spent on the houses was impressive.

His two-story red-brick house sat in the middle of a curved driveway. White pillars graced the front porch in plantation style. I parked in front of the double wide forest green doors. "I have a really bad feeling about this."

"Me, too." Dakota pushed open his car door. "I can see his jeep parked in the garage. It isn't like him not to come to work without telling me."

"Maybe you should stay in the car and let me check it out." I grabbed my pink Glock from my purse.

"Not a chance." He dug through my personal things until his hand came from the recesses of my purse clutching my Tazor.

My sister was going to kill me if anything happened to her almost seventeen-year-old son. "Then, at least stay behind me." *Please, God, don't let us die.*

I tried the front door. Locked. I led the way to the back door where the window in the kitchen door was shattered and the door swung open. "Be careful of the glass."

"I'm not a baby."

"Just saying."

I stepped into the kitchen, gun at the ready, and moved around the island until I found Mr. Dixon very, very dead. "Unfortunately, the video stream was real." I leaned against the counter. "I'm sorry, Dakota."

"Yeah, I really liked him." He glanced to where a camera was mounted in the corner above the cabinets. "I bet this house is loaded with cool things. One of these cameras had to have caught the killer in action."

"I agree. The chances of the police letting us anywhere near this place once they get here are slim, so…without touching anything…see what you can find out, and I'll wait for Wayne. No, nevermind. You stay here, and I'll look around." What if the killer was still there? I couldn't send Dakota into danger.

He paled. "Don't leave me with the body."

"Fine. We'll both go. Stay close to me."

The first room we stepped into was an office lined with computer monitors and book shelves. Instead of books, the shelves were filled with discs. Bingo. "Find the most current." I headed for the book shelf, Dakota for the computers.

"I doubt he's transferred the new stuff yet," he said, sitting at the desk. "I'm right. I'm going to save and then transfer to a jump drive, so we can let the cops find the information on their own."

"You're brilliant!" I leaned over his shoulder and watched the genius boy work.

Five minutes later, I heard soft steps coming down the hall. I held my gun back at the ready. "Hide the recording."

I cocked the gun and took my stance.

3

"Seriously, Stormi?" Officer Wayne Jones shook his head. "You really need to stop pointing your gun at me."

I lowered my weapon. "How did you know we were up here?"

"I heard you moving around. Stop snooping and get back downstairs. You're contaminating a crime scene."

Unfortunately, I heard that phrase way too often. I motioned my head at Dakota to follow Wayne and took a glance around the office to make sure we were leaving it as we found it.

"Hand it over." Wayne turned as soon as we entered the kitchen.

"What?"

"Whatever you found."

"We didn't have time to find anything. Not even the killer." I narrowed my eyes. "He, or she, might be hiding on the second floor. We didn't make it that far."

He made a noncommittal sound in his throat and turned his attention back to poor Mr. Dixon. "The authorities are on their way. Why don't the two of you have a seat so someone can take your statement?"

That, too, was an all too familiar phrase to my ears. I pulled out a chair at the table, Dakota doing the same next to me, and we watched Wayne punch in numbers on his phone as he walked around the body.

It felt strange to sit in a dead man's kitchen in the middle of the day. The harsh sun through the windows lit everything in glaring detail. I much preferred the scene seen through the television monitors at Gadgets and More. That scene was in black and white. Not that this was my first dead body, quite the contrary, but I definitely couldn't get used to the sight.

Sirens split the air outside. Minutes later, a flock of people wearing navy jackets, and Michael Barker, Maryann's squeeze, entered the kitchen.

Wayne barked a few orders, set the rookie Michael on the task of securing the scene, then sat across from me and Dakota. He pulled a small pad of paper from his shirt pocket and exhaled sharply. "You know the drill. Spill. Wait." He held up his index finger. "Matt has been gone an hour. You arrived home early this morning. How in the world did you get involved in a murder so quickly? Honestly, I'm baffled."

"That would be my fault," Dakota said, crossing his arms with a grin.

"You think this is funny, son? We have a dead man lying on the floor behind me."

His smile faded. "No, sir. I chose to forget that my boss is dead with a knife in his back."

"Explain how this is your fault." Wayne speared him with a sharp gaze.

"Mr. Dixon has, had, been acting strange the last week or so. I started following him and spying when he checked the security cameras at the store." He nodded at me. "I learned those things from Aunt Stormi. I'm her assistant, you know. Anyway, when I saw footage this morning of this kitchen and Mr. Dixon like…that, I texted Aunt Stormi to meet me at the store. She did. Then," he took a deep breath, "when we determined he wasn't playing a sick joke on me for spying on him, that he really was dead, we came here to check it out. Whew. That's it."

"Then, I called you," I said, not wanting to be left out of the interrogation. "We didn't touch the body, the weapon…nothing."

"You hesitated."

"No, I didn't."

He gave me 'the look'. "If you aren't honest with me, I'll have to call Matt."

"Why? I haven't done anything to warrant you bothering him while he's on what is possibly a dangerous assignment." Really, the man knew how to push my buttons. Other than bulging muscles, I didn't know what my sister saw in him.

"You're a horrible liar, Stormi. What did the two of you find?"

I took a deep breath, hoping I wouldn't let it slip that we'd taken a jump drive with the very information I was going to tell him about. "Dakota found the security footage from this morning on the computer, but you arrived before we could look at it."

"Barker! Go get the victim's computer. Now," he said, pushing up from the table, "that wasn't so hard, was it? Telling the truth?"

Dakota and I shook our heads like matching bobble head dolls.

"Good. Now go home before Angela has all our heads." He turned away, dismissing us.

Not being able to wait any longer to see what was on the jump drive, Dakota and I made a fast beeline for my car. "We might be able to solve this crime today." I slid into the driver's seat.

At home, we were in such a hurry to get to my office, we tried entering the room at the same time and were temporarily stuck. I laughed and stepped back. "You first. It's your case, after all."

"Case for what?" Mom stopped a few feet away, her arms loaded with folded laundry.

"I thought you went to Heavenly Bakes." Now, she'd want to know everything that had gone on that morning.

"I did. Greta has a good handle on things, so I came home to finish the laundry. What have you two been doing?"

I explained in as few words as possible while Dakota loaded the security footage onto my laptop. "Now, we want to see whether the killer was caught on film."

Mom dropped the laundry on a chair next to the desk and crowded next to me behind Dakota. "It sure didn't take us long to find a new mystery to solve."

"You have a business baking. I have a PI license and write books. Let's each stay to our own thing." Had she forgotten already that she'd almost died by a bullet? Mom was fifty. I couldn't let a woman of her age be in the same danger I seemed to be unable to avoid.

"You're thinking I'm old! I can see it

on your face." Mom frowned. "I'll have you know I've got a boyfriend."

"You do?" Dakota and I said in unison.

"Why haven't you said anything?" I asked.

She shrugged. "After the fiasco with Robert, I wanted to make sure Jerry wasn't doing anything illegal or shady. Matthew and Wayne checked him out for me and we went to dinner a few times while you were in Louisiana."

"When can I meet him?"

"When can you give him the third degree, you mean?" She lifted her chin. "He's coming to dinner tomorrow night."

"We're loaded." Dakota rolled back far enough from the computer screen so Mom and I could see.

The images were in black and white. Mr. Dixon mixed coffee grounds into a coffee pot, then leaned against his kitchen island while it perked. Something attracted his attention off to the side. His eyes widened, and he took a few steps away from what he was looking at.

With my heart in my throat, I watched

as a thin figure in black, wearing a ski mask, stepped into the camera's view.

Mr. Dixon shook his head, said something, then held up his hands in defense as the black clothed person charged. When Mr. Dixon turned to run, the killer plunged the knife into his back.

"My goodness." Mom staggered back. "He didn't even try to fight back."

"Yeah." We'd all seen the aftermath of murder, but I, for one, had never seen one take place.

Once Mr. Dixon was face down on the floor and no longer moving, the killer stepped back out of the camera's view. Then, for a reason we couldn't see, the person darted across the kitchen and out the back door.

"That could be anyone," Dakota said, turning off the computer. "I want to hire you, Aunt Stormi, to find out who killed my boss, why, and bring them to justice. I have three hundred dollars in my savings account."

"That's all?" Mom crossed her arms. "You're supposed to be saving for a car."

"I bought a few gadgets."

"Let's not stray off topic." I perched on the corner of my desk. "You don't have to pay me, Dakota. I'm involved in this now." After witnessing someone's death, there was nothing I wanted more, other than marrying Matt, than getting justice for the victim. "That killer could be anyone. I have no idea where to go from here."

I hopped off the desk and paced my office. "Did Mr. Dixon have any family? We need to find the reason someone would kill him." I chewed on my thumb nail. "Had he had any irate customers lately?"

Dakota shook his head. "Everyone loved him."

"Not everyone." Mom ruffled his hair. "Think, smart one. There has to be something that happened at that store."

"Sometimes, he rented his equipment to customers. Do you think maybe he saw something he shouldn't have?" Dakota glanced at me, then Mom. "Maybe someone didn't erase everything on the recording when they returned the stuff."

"It's as good a theory as any." The

problem would be finding out whether my nephew was on to something.

The doorbell rang. The three of us looked at each other.

"Let Angela get it." Mom glanced at her watch. "She should be home any minute."

"Someone left a box on the porch!" Angela yelled up the stairs.

Mom grinned. "See? That girl is predictable."

"The box is meowing!"

Strange, but better than ticking. I headed downstairs to where Angela stared at a box on the living room coffee table.

"There's no address label or anything," she said. "Should I open it?"

"If it is a cat, we can't leave the poor thing in the box." I grabbed a pair of scissors from the counter and slit the tape. I unfolded the box and peered into the face of a black kitten with yellow eyes. "Hello, cutie."

"Close it!" Angela slapped the box closed, then gathered it into her arms and headed for the back door.

"Wait. Stop. What are you doing?" I

grabbed her arm.

"It's a black cat, Stormi. An unknown person left it on your doorstep."

"So?"

She stared at me as if I'd grown a third eye. "This morning, you found a voodoo doll in your suitcase. Now, this cat."

I must be dense because I still didn't know where she was going with it. I shrugged.

"Voo. Doo. Duh. Someone is out to get you."

I didn't believe in such things, but my sister might have a point. Between the eerie gifts and Mr. Dixon's death, it looked as if I'd have plenty of things to do while Matt was gone.

The trick would be not getting killed while doing them.

4

"You aren't tossing the kitten out like garbage." I took the little darling from her and set it free in the house. Ebony and Ivory might not like little Midnight at first, but they'd get used to him or her. "I don't know of a single person who dabbles in such stupidity."

"We did just come from New Orleans. Who did you make mad while we were there?" She kept a wary eye on the kitten who attacked my shoelaces with playful vengeance.

"Nobody. I stayed with the group and minded my own—" Matt's ex. Would such a modern woman really rely on superstition to prevent me from marrying Matt? The Ozark country had its share of superstition steeped in tradition, but no one had thought to bother me with it before. "I have enough to worry about without playing games."

"The person sending you these things may not be playing." She took a wide berth around the kitchen in order to avoid Midnight and skedaddled up the stairs, calling out, "I can't live here if that cat stays! One black cat is enough."

"Ebony was here first and Midnight is a baby!"

"What's with all the yelling?" Mom made a beeline for the coffee pot. "Who is our new friend?"

"Someone dropped it off on the front porch. Angela thinks its voodoo."

"Really? Looks like a kitten to me." Mom dumped the old remaining bit of coffee down the sink and filled the pot with fresh water. "It's going to be a long day. Greta just called. We got in a rush order for some big corporate party. Don't wait up for me."

"Okay." I'd be occupied trying to figure out who had a reason to kill Mr. Dixon. "Don't make coffee for me. I'm heading over to Delicious Aroma."

"Good idea. If anyone knows anything about what's going on around town, Norma will."

I agreed. My former prostitute friend turned business owner seemed to know almost everything that went on in Oak Meadows. Folks in town liked to talk over their coffee, and Norma had good ears. Plus, no matter how sexy she dressed, she miraculously disappeared when sitting at the back corner table with her laptop and accounting books opened.

Suddenly struck with emotion over yet another dangerous mystery, I wrapped my mother in a hug and kissed her cheek. "Wake me when you get home if I'm in bed."

"I love you, too, dear." Mom patted my cheek. "Now, go find a killer, but save some of the fun for me."

I stopped by my office looking for Dakota. Not finding him, I headed up the stairs to his bedroom. I knocked on the door. When he didn't answer, I walked in.

"Aunt Stormi!" He bent over something on the floor. "Knock first.

What if I were naked?"

"Nothing I haven't seen before, and I did knock. What are you hiding?"

He sighed and straightened to reveal some very high tech looking equipment. "What I've spent my paychecks on."

"Which is?"

"Recording and surveillance equipment. What I let you use when Cherokee was kidnapped was nothing compared to this stuff. Seriously, we could open up our own office."

"What are you doing with it now?"

"I'm going to try and hack into Mr. Dixon's computer files."

Impressive. "I like the way you think. I won't tell your mother. While you work on that, I'm heading downtown to talk to Norma. Is Cherokee at work?"

He nodded and continued hooking this line with that. I was effectively dismissed. No problem. I'd rather he snooped from the safety of his room than out on the street.

I really didn't know about my new need to say goodbye to my family before leaving the house. Maybe Angela's talk of voodoo had spooked me more than I thought.

Grabbing my purse from the foyer table, I set the alarm on the front door and headed to my car. Less than ten minutes later, I was parked in front of the coffee shop. Before I got out of the car, Mom had pulled behind me at the bakery. We tossed each other a wave and went into our prospective shops.

"Welcome back," Tyler, Norma's son called out the moment I stepped inside. "Your usual coming right up. Mom's in her office today. She's feeling a little down."

Maybe talking about a new crime would cheer her up. I headed for the back of the shop and knocked on the door marked 'Manager'.

"Come in."

I poked my head in. "It's me. Heard you were down and came to pick your brain."

"That's a scary thought. Too much going on in there." She waved at an empty chair in front of her desk.

"What's up?" I set my purse on her

desk and speared her with a stern gaze.

Her eyes welled with tears. "It's so silly. I feel like a girl in high school where the girl from the wrong side of the tracks has a crush on the star quarterback."

Uh-oh. "I didn't know you were interested in a relationship."

"I thought it was time. My past life has been just that…my past life, for a long time."

"And this man found out what you used to do."

"Yeah."

I stretched across the desk and put my hand on hers. "You'll find the right guy, Norma. Just give it time. There's a man out there now who will love you for you, not what happened a long time ago."

"Maybe." She snatched a tissue from a nearby box and wiped her eyes. "Your turn."

I explained about Mr. Dixon and what we saw on the tape. "Have you heard anything?"

"Come here." She opened the door and pointed to the counter. "See that new girl?"

"Yeah."

"She's…was…dating him. Her name is Jordyn Townsend. She keeps to herself."

"Any sign that something is up today?"

"Nope." Norma closed the door. "She probably doesn't know yet."

"She seems too pretty to date an old man like Dixon." Still, I'd seen, and heard, stranger things.

"Well, I don't judge my employees by their personal lives," Norma said, resuming her seat, "but I've heard the girl gets around. That Dixon might not have been the only name in her rolodex, if you get my drift."

I got it loud and clear. The gal serving coffee with Tyler might look like the girl next door with her bouncy ponytail and fresh skin, but looks were often deceiving. Take Norma for instance. She might not be a hooker any longer, but she still had a heavy hand with the makeup and showed more cleavage than me and Angela put together. Still, I'd never met a nicer person and was proud to call her friend.

"Do you think she's a killer?"

"No." Norma smiled. "But Mr. Dixon did a lot of side work spying on people. Find out who his customers were, and I'll bet one of them killed him. He probably saw something he shouldn't have."

"That's exactly what I thought."

Tyler entered without knocking and handed me my drink. "Jordyn is driving me crazy." He backed out of the room and slammed the door.

Norma grinned. "That's one boy she can't seem to charm. They've clashed since day one."

"She doesn't have enough facial piercings for your son and is at least ten years older."

She laughed. "You're probably the only person I'd allow to say something like that about my baby's fashion sense."

I returned her grin. "I say it with love. Let me know if you hear anything of interest, okay? I've got a wedding to plan. Solving a murder wasn't on my long list of things to do."

"Sometimes, life, or death, gets in the way," she said.

I knew that first hand. "What do you know about voodoo?"

"Not much." She cocked her head. "But, there is an old woman in the mountains who is rumored to be some kind of priestess. You might want to ask about her at the thrift store. I think her granddaughter works there. Think African princess."

"Thanks." Now, I really was sure I wanted nothing to do with voodoo nonsense. A priestess on the mountain, an African princess...what else?

"Here." Norma handed me a cross necklace. "It's been blessed."

"Oooo-kay." I took the jewelry and dropped it into my purse. The cross had to be five inches long and weighed a ton. "I'll talk to you later. Keep your chin up."

"You keep the bad ju-ju off your back."

Her ominous words followed me all the way to the car. Few things shook my faith, but between Angela and Norma, things were trembling a bit. I needed a cupcake to go with my coffee, so I headed across the street to Mom's bakery. Greta was an ex-cop. Maybe she knew something about all this nonsense that could help me.

"Welcome to Heavenly—oh, hello, dear." Mom wiped her hands on a towel. "How's the crime solving going?"

"Your mom told me about Mr. Dixon," Greta said, standing next to Mom. "A real shame."

I pushed through the waist high swinging doors that separated the front of the store from where the magic happened and grabbed a chocolate cupcake with chocolate frosting. "I've more than one mystery staring me in the face. There's Mr. Dixon and now, it seems as if someone is trying to give me the evil eye." I told them about the doll, the cat, and the old lady on the mountain. "Would you know anything about anything happening around here, Greta?"

"There are still a few old timers that believe in that stuff, but it seems to be dying off with them." She handed me a napkin. "Thank the Lord in Heaven."

"Do you know anything about the new barista, Jordyn?" I took a big bite and rolled my eyes with pleasure.

"She's a bit of a floozy, just like her mother was, bless her heart, or so the rumors go. She isn't from around here. The mother's dead now. Been gone about ten years. Drug overdose. That's what I heard." Greta leaned close as if there were someone around to hear. "Some say it was done to her. You know? Like a Marilyn Monroe type of thing."

Things were now sounding like a conspiracy theory. "Please tell me you agree that these two things are not related. Because, if they are, I'm afraid my nephew is going to be very disappointed. I am not going to investigate a death where the devil had played." I shoved the last of the cupcake in my mouth.

"I don't think they're related." Greta measured flour into a large stainless steel bowl. "But, I do think you need to be careful."

"Not that either of you asked," Mom said, "but I think you need to call Matthew and tell him his ex-fiance is playing dirty."

5

I woke the next morning to my phone ringing. I grappled on the nightstand for it, elated to see Matt's number. "Hello."

"Good morning, gorgeous." His deep voice sent shivers up my spine, and not in a bad way. "How are you?"

"I'm great, now that you've called. You?"

"I'm doing okay. Should be home in a few days. What are you doing today?"

Uh-oh. I could tell from the tone of his voice that he'd spoken with someone who had filled him in on some of the details. Wayne Jones had loose lips! "Your girlfriend is sending me scary gifts!" Well, not necessarily all scary. I grinned as Midnight attacked my toes under the sheets while Sadie and the other two cats watched.

"Ex-girlfriend. What is she doing?"

I explained about the doll and cat. "I think she's harmless and just expressing her displeasure, but Angela thinks she's trying to curse me."

"Ignore Rachel and your sister. I'll take care of that. Now, about Mr. Dixon…"

I spilled my guts, even going as far as letting him know about Dakota downloading the recording. "Today, I'm going to visit some old voodoo lady on the mountain while Dakota sets up his spy equipment."

"I said I'd take care of Rachel's nonsense."

"Are you a voodoo expert?"

"Well, no—"

"Supposedly, this woman is. I just want to make sure I don't need to expect your ex to lean over me with a knife while I'm sleeping." Why couldn't the woman have stayed at some exotic locale taking her photographs?

"That won't happen." He sighed.

"You need to be more worried about who killed Dixon. Why do you get involved in these things when I'm gone?"

I couldn't tell him that losing him was my biggest fear. That had come toot close to happening with the last two mysteries. "Dakota asked for my help. After seeing the tape, I can't back out. You know that."

"Yes, I do. Please, be careful. Investigate from behind the scenes and let the police do any confronting. I'd like you alive to marry me in a couple of months."

I smiled. "Me, too. I'm going to pick up my dress today after I visit the mountain."

"I love you. See you in a few."

"I love you, too." We hung up and I got out of bed to face the day. A quick call to Maryann to see whether she wanted to go with me—she did—and I headed for the shower.

Thirty minutes later, I'd picked up my maid-of-honor and second-in-command at solving crime, stopped for coffee, and headed to the thrift store to find an African princess.

"Speaking of voodoo," I said, turning

off the car's ignition, "did you dump the syrup in Michael's drink?"

"Yeah." Her shoulders slumped. "No proposal."

I laughed. "Give it time. The man loves you. A blind person can see it."

"Really?"

"Really."

We entered the thrift store and peered past the miles of shelves filled with dusty things. The counter close to the door was empty of all but a cash register. We could have easily grabbed the thing and dashed back out.

"Be right there." A throaty voice from somewhere behind a rack of clothes stated. When the woman appeared, there was no doubting why Norma described her the way she had. The store proprietor wore ethnic clothes in rich browns, greens, and gold. She easily stood five foot ten or taller. The hair piled high on her head made her a giant. She grinned, her teeth startling white against her ebony skin. I'd never seen a more striking woman. "Are you looking for something in particular?"

"Voodoo," Maryann blurted out. She gasped and clasped a hand over her mouth.

"Let me guess. Unrequited love." The Amazon glided behind the counter. "I don't practice black magic."

"Ignore her." I stepped in front of Maryann. "Why would two very white Christian women be interested in such things?"

"I've been receiving some…well, some people think they're threats. A doll and a black cat. I don't believe in such things, as you say, but I'd like to talk to the old woman on the mountain to see whether I should be alarmed?"

"Oh, you should be alarmed, all right. Black magic is never anything to scoff at, as Mamba Jane will tell you. Here." She drew a rough map on the back of a slip of register tape. "You tell her Sissy sent you. That way…she won't shoot you."

"Wow. Thanks." I grabbed Maryann's arm and got out of there as fast as possible. "What is wrong with you?"

"I choked. She's very intimidating."

I rolled my eyes. "Don't say a word at

Mamba Jane's. Let me do the talking. Your brother would prefer I stay alive."

She nodded. "I completely agree." She buckled her seatbelt. "Onward."

According to the map, we took Eagle Hill Road and wound our way to the top. A rarely traveled dirt road with nothing more than a rusty antique milk can as a marker took us to the right. The car bottomed out several times in potholes as big as bath tubs.

"We're walking." I cut the ignition. "I'm not going to damage my car."

"According to the map, we have a couple of miles." Maryann frowned.

I glanced at her feet, glad to see we'd both had the foresight to wear gym shoes instead of flip flops. "Toughen up. We can do this." I shoved open my door and stepped into a thick forest. A quick glance at my phone showed I had no cell phone service. Great. I said a quick prayer for protection and set off down the road with Maryann rushing to catch up.

"We don't have any food or water," she said.

"I don't plan on spending the night."

"I'm a hard working literary assistant and crime solver," she said, panting. "But hiking is not my thing."

"Think of it as an adventure."

"Ugh."

An hour later, I wasn't thinking so fondly of our so-called adventure either, but we had arrived at our destination. In front of us was a log cabin, the type you might see in a magazine. Smoke drifted lazily from the chimney despite the warm autumn day.

"It doesn't look like a witch's house," Maryann said.

"Who said anything about her being a witch?"

"Are you afraid?"

"No."

"Then why aren't you knocking on the door?"

Good question. Maybe I was a little fearful. Experience had taught me things were not always as welcoming as they may seem. I took a deep breath and climbed the three steps leading to the front door. I rapped three times and stepped back.

"Who's there?" A voice as full and throaty as the Amazon's said.

"We were sent by Sissy."

The door swung open. A little old lady with a wrinkled face and hunched back stared out at us. "What you want?"

"I have a couple of questions."

"We should have brought the doll," Maryann whispered.

"What doll?" Mamba Jane's eyes narrowed.

I explained about the doll and cat. "What should I do?"

"I could sell you a gris gris to ward off evil spirits," she said. "But, it seems more like someone is toying with you. No fear."

"They aren't warning me that they want me dead?"

"Out of picture, yes, dead...probably not. You want buy something?"

I shook my head. It looked as if Maryann and I had wasted our time. Except for the fact that despite my saying I wasn't superstitious, I felt a lot better. "Thank you for answering our questions."

Mamba Jane's eyes widened. "Maybe

giver of doll not harm you, but harm will come. Oh, yes. You be careful and wear that cross." She slammed the door.

"What cross?" Maryann said.

"Norma gave me one as a good luck charm."

"Where is it?"

"In my purse in the car." My real good luck charm, God, was always with me. "I'm not going to run scared on the words of an old woman. No one even knows I'm working on Dixon's murder case."

"But somebody will." She wagged her finger in my face. "They always find out. How did she know you had a cross in your purse?"

I didn't want to think about that. "Let's go pick up my wedding dress." We both needed something fun to overshadow the warning of Mamba Jane.

~

Two hours later, I stood in front of enough full length mirrors to see every side of me. My form fitting gown with a kick out hem made me feel like a queen. The cathedral veil splayed out behind me.

"You're gorgeous in that." Maryann's eyes shimmered. "Wait until Matt sees you."

I glanced at her royal blue knee length sheath style dress. "That is the perfect color for you."

She sighed. "Getting married at the lake with autumn leaves raining down on you will be beautiful. The water will sparkle behind you. It's perfect."

"I hope so. Help me out of this so we can get it home and in the closet." Out of harm's way of four inquisitive pets. Midnight would most likely see it as a climbing opportunity. "We need to run by the bakery. Greta wants me to show her the dress."

"Around all that chocolate?"

"I'll have her come out to the car." I grinned and lifted my hair so Maryann could work the zipper.

"I sincerely hope that dress is one of a kind."

I turned to see Rachel, arms crossed, a simpering smile on her face.

"What are you doing here?" I asked.

"I was running errands and saw the

two of you pop in, so I thought I'd follow." She made a slow circle around me. She didn't say anything, but I knew she found me lacking somewhere.

"Go away, Rachel." Maryann pulled aside the curtain to the dressing room. "You can't stop this wedding. Matt loves Stormi in a way he never cared for you."

High spots of color appeared on the other woman's cheeks. "It was I who broke off the engagement," she said with a toss of her head. "It is I who can win him back." With a toss of flowing locks, she whirled and marched away.

"Don't believe a word she says, Stormi." Maryann let the curtain fall in place after I stepped in. "You're Matt's world."

I knew that, but Rachel's words still stole some of the joy of the occasion. I shimmied, my dress puddling at my feet, and stared at my body in the mirror. Full bosom, although not large, a tiny waist, lean hips. I could hold my own, I decided. Even against a woman as curvy as Rachel.

I hung the dress on the hanger, covered it with the thick plastic protective bag, and then rejoined Maryann. "Let's go home."

We stopped by the bakery and let Mom and Greta ooh and ahh over my dress, then pack us a box of finger cookies to take home. Something new they were trying, Mom said.

I explained to them about our morning adventure and seeing Rachel at the dress shop. "I should have asked her if she really is the one sending me stuff like the doll and cat. Although, I think of Midnight more as a gift. But I was in shock to see her at the wedding shop and forgot."

"I did a bit of background checking on her while you were gone." Greta snatched a sheet of paper from next to the computer. "Seems our little Rachel lost her job last month for fooling around with a married co-worker."

And, she saw Matt as her way back to respectability.

6

At home, I hung my wedding dress in my closet and headed for Dakota's lair...uh, room. This time I knocked, then knocked again, before he told me to enter.

"Mr. Dixon has a daughter," Dakota said, not looking up from his computer. "Strange that he never mentioned her, but she lives on the outskirts of town." He printed off a sheet of paper and handed it to me. "Her address."

"You're a marvel, oh, favorite nephew of mine." I ruffled his hair. "Let me know if you find anything else of interest. I need to write down what I've learned so far...in story form...so my agent doesn't have a coronary."

He didn't acknowledge that I'd

spoken. "I'm going to take a few days off of school to work on this."

"No, you're not. You didn't go today, I'm assuming. You'll have to do your spying after school. It wouldn't hurt for you to look for a new job, either."

That got his attention. He jerked his gaze away from the computer. "Aren't you going to pay me for being your tech guy?"

This was news to me. "If I do, you realize it won't be every day work unless someone hires me, right?"

"That's fine. I don't have any expenses."

I shrugged and headed for my office. It wasn't the first time my sister was going to want to kill me because of my relationship with her kids. I tended to be a very lenient aunt.

At my desk, I booted up my computer. Sure enough, there was an email from my agent wanting to know details on my next book. I sent off a quick reply that I was just starting a doozy. Then, not to be a liar, I started my story with Rachel in Louisiana, only I changed the name of the not-so-innocent.

Two hours later, I had the rough draft of the first chapter, ending with Dakota's text to me. I stretched, popping kinks from my back, and rolled my chair back. When I was writing, I tended to forget to eat and drink. Now, my stomach grumbled and my mouth felt like it was filled with cotton.

Maryann glanced up from the kitchen table when I entered. "Everything is set for your book signing tomorrow."

I'd forgotten. "I hate those things."

"They're necessary for you to connect with your readers. Are you hungry? I ordered a pizza."

"You're the best assistant ever." I opened the fridge, grabbed a bottle of strawberry flavored water and sat across from her. "Dakota seems to think he's my tech guy and expects payment."

"You can afford it."

"True, but if this keeps up, I might have to actually advertise the fact that I'm a licensed private investigator." I unscrewed the lid on the bottle and took several big gulps. Ah, that was better.

"You have a lot on your plate." She closed her laptop. "You write three books a year, solve mysteries so you have material for those three books, and got your license so you could have access to places you wouldn't otherwise. Why do you have to hire yourself out?"

"I don't know. Seems like a waste of a license if I don't." I grinned.

"I think Matt expects to get you pregnant as soon as possible so you'll stop your gumshoeing."

I had just taken another drink and ended up spewing the water across the table. "He said that?" I wanted children of my own, I really did. Yes, I'd give up solving mysteries for them. "What would I write about?"

"You'll go back to making stuff up."

True. It was harder that way, but a whole lot safer. "Want to go visit Mr. Dixon's daughter?"

"Sure. I'm finished here."

I texted Dakota to let him know we were leaving, grabbed my purse, then headed for my car, Maryann behind me. I felt good at having carved out writing time in addition to doing more snooping. Unfortunately, solving crime sometimes pushed writing aside. This morning reinforced how much I enjoyed creating a story, whether based on fact or fiction.

I drove us to a small suburb on the south side of town and drove slowly until I found the address Dakota had given me. No vehicle sat parked in front of the 1980s style house or in the carport. All curtains were drawn on the windows.

"It doesn't look as if anyone is home," Maryann said.

"No, it doesn't. I'll go ring the doorbell, just in case." I opened my door and marched to the front door. I rang the doorbell and waited. Nothing. Cupping my hands around my eyes, I tried peering through the front curtains.

"She ain't home."

I turned to see a woman in a floral housedress come around the corner of the house next door. She carried a garden hose.

"Do you know when she'll be home?" I asked.

"She don't give me her schedule."

The woman glared, hooking the hose to the faucet and turning on the water. "She works over at the diner on 64. Maybe you should ask her yourself, iffen you're brave enough to step foot into that place."

"Thank you." I hurried back to the car before the woman could turn the hose on me. "Do you know of a diner on 64?" I asked Maryann as soon as I returned to the safety of the car.

"Yeah, it's a real dive. More like a biker bar than a diner. It's called Steak and Leather."

"Well, put on your leather and studs. We're going to a biker bar."

She groaned. "I've heard there's a shooting or stabbing there at least once a week."

"I doubt it happens on a Friday afternoon." At least, I hoped not. I headed the car toward our new destination, again praying for our safety. God must have a huge storage container to hold all of my prayers of safety. In our skinny jeans and long-sleeved tee shirts, Maryann and I didn't look the least like biker chicks.

I parked across from a line of

motorcycles in every color and model I'd ever heard of. A couple of men leaned against the wood shingle sided building and smoked cigarettes. I licked dry lips and waited to muster up the courage to get out of the car.

"We can do this," I said. "We've been in worse situations. I've heard that once a biker is your friend, then they're the nicest people you'll ever meet."

"They aren't our friends."

"Let's hope we can get them to be." I pushed open my door and stepped onto the gravel parking lot. How did one become friends with such scary looking people?

The two smokers watched our progression to the swinging front doors without saying a word. When we stepped into the dim recesses of the bar, all conversation stopped and all heads turned in our direction. Two women in baby blue dresses and white aprons served those sitting at scarred round tables. A long polished bar stretched the full length of one end of the building. At the opposite end, a blinking red sign showed folks where the bathrooms were.

"You two ladies lost?" The bartender grinned, somehow making the word 'ladies' sound like a dirty word.

I bellied up to the bar, or so the saying goes. "We're looking for April Dixon."

"We got one April here, and she don't go by the name of Dixon. You a cop?"

"No, I'm an author."

"Hey!" A burly man with a full beard that fell halfway down his chest approached at full speed.

I shrieked and pressed against the bar.

Maryann ducked under a table.

"You're Stormi Nelson," the man said. "I've read all your books. You here for research?"

I relaxed, exhaling heavily. "Kind of."

"I'm Ben Haverson." He thrust out a meaty paw. "You want to talk to April? Hey, April, get your skinny rear over here and talk to my friend." He bent close, covering me with tobacco scented breath. "You ever need anything, Stormi Nelson, anything at all, you call on Ben. I'll get my buddies and come to your rescue." He thrust a business card into my hand.

A business card? Could the day get any stranger? "Thank you."

He grinned and headed back to a table where he sat and pointed me out to the other three men sitting there.

"Wow." Maryann crawled from under the table. "You just made friends with a biker. You have all the luck."

"If you hadn't have ran off like a scaredy-cat, maybe you'd be his friend, too."

"What do you want?" A rail-thin woman about thirty years old with Lucille Ball red hair propped a metal tray on her hip.

"Is your father the Dixon who owns Gadgets and More?"

Her lip curled. "I don't acknowledge him, but for the sake of your questions, yes."

"Were you aware he was murdered yesterday?"

A flicker of pain crossed her features. "What's that got to do with me?"

"I'm a private investigator trying to find his killer. Please, can we sit down and talk?"

She glanced around me at the bartender. "Roy?"

"Take all the time you need," he said. "Sorry about your father. Use my office."

April nodded. "Follow me." She set the tray on the bar and led us down a short hall to a room at the end. If not for my new friend, Ben, I'd be nervous entering the bowels of such a place.

She sat in a chair patched with duct tape and waved us toward two mismatched wooden chairs. Mine had one leg shorter than the others. "I'm all ears."

"My nephew worked for your father and never knew he had a daughter." I tried not to let the chair wiggle. "That leads me to believe you're estranged?"

"I have no use for a man who will cheat on my mother, then build a business helping others catch cheating spouses. Too little, too late, in my opinion. So, after my mother's death a few years ago, I legally changed my name to Brown." She grinned. "Plain and simple."

"So you have no idea why someone would want your father dead?"

"I'm sure a lot of people wanted him dead." She crossed her arms. "There are people out there who don't take kindly to folks butting into their business. You might want to check out his new little girlfriend."

The new barista was next on my list. "Do you know how we might be able to find out where his files are located so we can see a list of his clients?"

She thought for a moment. "He never told me his secrets, but when I was a kid, he hid any valuables we might have under the floor. Check out his office. He's bound to have a similar hiding place."

"Thank you." I handed her one of my PI cards. "Please call me if you think of anything else that might help me, and I'm sorry for your loss."

She shrugged. "The world is less one more low-life. I'm more sorry for your nephew for having worked for my father."

"He was kind to my nephew."

"Maybe he changed after my mother's death. She committed suicide, you know? Three weeks after he left her."

I probably wouldn't want to speak

with him again either. I missed my own father with a never-ending ache and always carried the hope with me that someday I might catch his killer. While I waited, I brought justice and closure to others.

"Dixon had some secrets, it seems," I said, making my way back to the main room.

"Sounds like it. So…when do you want to break the law and enter the crime scene?" Maryann grinned.

"Tonight. Under the cover of darkness." I waved at Ben and headed into the afternoon sunshine.

All I needed to figure out at that moment was how to sneak out of the house without my mother knowing. Snooping at night was one of her favorite things to do.

I stopped short. Tonight was dinner with Mom's new boyfriend. I'd have my entire family to dodge. I called Maryann and told her to meet me in front of her house at eleven p.m.

7

I wore the same pair of jeans for dinner that I'd worn that day, but did put on a pretty black blouse. I might not have time to change before meeting Maryann and needed to be in dark clothes.

Mom's eyes narrowed the moment I entered the kitchen. "Are you in mourning because of meeting Jerry?"

"No." Was she serious? "Don't you like this blouse? You gave it to me for Christmas."

"I don't remember giving you anything black." She turned back to the stove. "Would you mind making the salad? All the fixings are on the island. This baked spaghetti is almost done and I need to start on the bread."

"I'd love to." I cut her a sideways glance. She sure was nervous about this guy. More so than I'd ever seen her. "You must really like Jerry."

A slow smile spread across her face. "I do. He's handsome, kind, and a Godly man. He's the best, next to your father." Her smiled faded. "I haven't told him how I help you solve crimes, so no mention of that tonight, understand?"

I pretended to lock my lips and throw away the key. "Does that mean you're finished helping me?"

"It does not. It only means that it is too early in the relationship for him to know I do dangerous things. He thinks I'm sweet and feminine."

I laughed. "He'll find out that's a lie soon enough without me saying anything."

The doorbell rang. Mom gasped and removed her apron, hanging it on a hook. She patted her hair. "How do I look?"

I ran my gaze over her red dress with black paisley print. "Gorgeous. Go knock him out."

She grinned and hurried to answer the

door, returning minutes later with a tall, fit, handsome man in his mid-fifties with salt and pepper hair. I swore he could be George Clooney's brother.

"It's nice to meet you, Jerry. I'm Stormi, Mom's youngest." I wiped my hand on my jeans and held it out to him.

"The pleasure is mine." His deep voice rumbled through the room.

Oh, I hoped this worked out for Mom. She deserved a man like this. At least if first impressions were accurate to how wonderful he was.

"Why don't the two of you have a seat in the living room? I can finish up here. Send Angela down to help me." I waved them away.

"Thank you, sweetie." Mom linked her arm with Jerry's. "I can't wait for you to meet the rest of the family."

Seeing them together made me miss my man. I fought the urge to call him. He'd told me the first time that if I called and he was in surveillance mode, I could give him away. So, no matter how much I needed him, I refrained from calling and waited for him to call me. I sighed and tossed the cherry tomatoes I'd rinsed on top of the salad.

"Mom said you need help." Angela sashayed into the room wearing a dress so tight it looked painted on. I hoped my figure held up after two kids...if I ever had them. "Wayne is coming, so I can only help until he arrives."

"I'll put him to work."

She shook her head. "Nope. I hardly ever get to spend time with him. I'm going to steal a few minutes, if I can. I'll send Cherokee in, if I have to. That girl takes forever to get ready. A chore to do will hurry her up."

Or make her dawdle longer. I shrugged. It was only dinner at home, not a fancy restaurant. "I can handle dinner, then." Salad finished, I grabbed the bread knife and sliced the fresh loaf of sourdough Mom had baked. No store bought bread in this house.

By the time I heard feet thundering down the stairs, I had dinner complete and the dining room table set. Forget any help. I'd probably be stuck cleaning up, too. I carried the food to the table. "Time to eat!"

"Gracious." Mom entered the room with Jerry, her face red. "You'll have to excuse my youngest. I guess she forgot her manners."

"Sorry, but the dinner bell is broken."

Angela sat next to Wayne whose arrival I'd missed. "She's just mad because I couldn't help her with dinner. You'll find my sister is quite a pouter, Jerry."

"You'll also find that sibling rivalry runs rampant in this house." Mom narrowed her eyes at us as Jerry pulled out her chair.

"No problem here. My two boys end up breaking something every time they come home for a visit together." He grinned and sat next to Mom, leaving me at one end of the table.

Dakota shrugged and took the other end where Mom usually sat and Cherokee sat next to me. "You aren't a killer, a thief, an embezzler or a sex trafficker, are you?" Dakota asked. "Because, we've had enough of those."

"Oh, for heaven's sake." Mom's face

got darker.

Wayne laughed and grabbed his water glass. "You'll find life is never boring around this family. Don't worry, Dakota. I checked Jerry out for you."

"You did?" Jerry cocked his head. "Glad to know this family has someone like you looking out for them."

"Wait until you meet my fiancé." I wasn't about to let Matt be left out. "He's wonderful."

"Did Grandma tell you that we're investigating my boss's death?" Dakota was full of information that evening.

"Excuse me?" Jerry glanced at Mom.

She sighed. "Stormi isn't only a novelist. She's also a private investigator, and we quite often help the local police solve murders. There. I said it."

"Against our better judgment," Wayne added. "But these women do have good insight."

"You catch killers." Jerry tucked his tongue into his cheek.

I got the suspicion he was trying not to laugh.

"Anne, you are a marvel." He

grabbed her hand and kissed it. "I am a lucky man."

"You aren't mad?"

"Heck, no. I might even join you on one of your adventures."

Mom beamed.

I rolled my eyes and reached for a slice of garlic bread. The last thing we needed was one more person involved and in the way.

~

While the others sipped wine or other drinks of choice in the living room, I pulled a dark beanie over my red hair and slipped out the back door at five minutes to eleven. I raced down the sidewalk to see Maryann, also in black, waiting at the curb.

"You'll have to drive," I said. "If I started up my car, Mom would hear, and the whole gang is over there."

"Right." She dashed back into her house and returned with car keys dangling from her fingers. "If Wayne is busy at your house, we'll be free and clear at Dixon's place."

"Where's Michael?"

"On duty." She grinned and slid behind the steering wheel. "It's perfect. Now, turn your phone to vibrate in case Matt calls."

"You think someone will be there to hear my phone?" I clicked my seatbelt across my lap. "I seriously doubt that. We're the only ones delinquent enough to disregard crime scene tape to enter the house."

"Well, someone has to do it." She backed from the drive and sped toward Dixon's house. "There are a couple of flashlights under the seat."

She parked a couple of houses down from his. "Let's do this."

I studied the yellow crime scene tape fluttering in the slight breeze. "Step over or duck under. Don't knock the tape down. I don't want any evidence that we were here," I told her as we approached the house. "Don't turn on your flashlight until we're inside." I led her around back.

The door was locked.

"See if he hides a key out here."

"You really think a man with so much surveillance equipment would actually hide a key outside?"

"Not really." I glanced at a small open bathroom window and had a flashback to my first night as Neighborhood Watch president. That great idea fizzled out within a few months. No one seemed willing to give up their evenings to patrol the neighborhood. Still, I got my dog out of the deal and met Matt. "Give me a boost."

Maryann stepped between two juniper bushes and cupped her hands. "Hurry. I'm not very strong."

I stepped on and lunged for the windowsill. I landed halfway in the window with the frame cutting into my stomach. "Give me a push."

She shoved against my rear end, sending me headfirst to the bathroom floor. I saw stars, and my foot landed in the toilet. Grace was not my middle name. I sincerely hoped it had been flushed before Dixon was killed. I got to my feet and sloshed my way down the hall, clicking on my flashlight, and opened the back door.

"You're bleeding." Maryann pointed

at my head.

"You shoved too hard. My forehead hit the tile." I pressed my hand against the lump. "I'll take care of it later. Let's find the loose floorboard." Nope. Needed to wipe up my DNA before anything else. I grabbed a wad of toilet paper, rubbed the blood off the floor, and tossed it in the toilet. A flush later and the evidence was gone.

We headed for Dixon's office. All computer equipment had been removed, leaving the room bare except for empty shelves.

"I'll start at this end, you start at that, and test every inch of the floor." I shoved against the desk. "Even under the furniture."

The desk rolled on casters. I grinned. The night might not be as long as I'd thought. I dropped to my knees and felt around the floor. There. A small indentation big enough for my fingers. I pulled up, revealing a small one by two section of removable wood paneling. "Bingo!"

Maryann peered over my shoulder.

"What's in there?"

I pulled out a large square metal box. "I'm thinking it's his client files." I opened the box and pulled out several sheets of paper with names, addresses, and phone numbers. "Is the copy machine still here?"

"Yes, they took the printer, though."

I got to my feet and made my way to the corner of the room. "We'll copy these, then turn the box over to Wayne." I was quite proud of myself. Once upon a time, I wouldn't have thought to share information with the police, but now that they've given up on keeping me out of their investigations, short of arresting me, I felt more inclined to share.

I made two copies of the papers, put the originals back in the hole in the floor and folded one set of the copies so they'd fit in my waistband. I gave the other set to Maryann, who did the same. "Easy. Let's go home."

Headlights illuminated the window.

We ducked and froze.

"Who is it?" Maryann asked.

"How should I know? But, if they're

here this late, it can't be good."

"Have I ever mentioned how dangerous being your literary assistant is?"

"A few times." I duck-walked to the door and peered into the hall. "I don't see anyone."

"Well, I see you." A flashlight clicked on and blinded me.

"That's rude, Wayne." I got to my feet. "You scared us."

"You shouldn't be here." He turned on the office light. "I figured when you weren't there for dessert that you were up to something. This is the only thing I could think of. What did you find?"

I pointed out the hole in the floor. "His daughter told us we might find something like that."

He retrieved the box. "Did you make copies?"

"Noooo." I shook my head at Maryann.

"Sure, you didn't." He shrugged. "Well, you'll be Matt's problem tomorrow. He's coming home."

I clapped my hands. "Great. Let's

go."

"I want those copies."

"I said, I don't have any."

"You're lying."

"Whatever." I pulled them from under my shirt. "Here. Happy?"

"Yes." He grinned and motioned for us to go ahead of him. "I promised Matt I'd keep you out of trouble. You sure make it hard on a guy. Angela is fuming because I left. Now, I've got to take these to the station before heading back to your house and turning her frown into a smile."

"Just lock them in your trunk. No one knows about them but us." I winked at Maryann and sailed into the hall. I'd gotten one over on Wayne. My night was complete.

8

The next morning, dressed in one of my only suits, black with a scarlet blouse, I headed to the bookstore in Little Rock for my signing. I parked in front of the store and grinned. Standing out front clutching a dozen red roses was my man.

I turned off the engine, shoved open my door, and ran as fast as my three inch heels would allow. "You're back."

He wrapped his free arm around me and pulled me close, landing his lips on mine. "With flowers." He straightened and handed me the roses. "Good luck with your signing. There's a line already forming inside."

"I hate these things." I took the roses and breathed deeply of their sweet scent.

"Not the roses, the signing."

"I know. That's why I'm here to give moral support. Maryann is at your table right now making sure you have plenty of books available for purchase. You have five minutes before your signing begins."

I slipped my hand in his. "I'd better get moving, then."

Sure enough, the line leading to my table was over twenty deep. Whispers and pointing fingers followed me to my assigned seat. I clutched Matt's hand harder and forced a smile on my face.

Maryann handed me my favorite signing pen. "Have fun and let me know if I need to get you anything." She reached under the table and retrieved my favorite coffee, then placed my roses in a crystal vase.

"You think of everything."

"That's why I quit teaching, and you pay me the big bucks to wait on you hand and foot." She smiled and stepped to the side.

My cheeks hurt and my hand started to cramp within half an hour. I did my best to only spend a couple of minutes with each customer, but still those waiting were straining their necks to see around those in front of them. I sighed and held out my hand for the next book.

"I'm not here to get you to sign anything."

I glanced up, my smile fading, and stared into the face of Rachel. "Good morning. If you aren't here to purchase a book, I'll have to ask you to step aside." I motioned for Maryann to find Matt. "Or perhaps, you'd like a complimentary copy."

She planted her hands flat on the table and leaned close to my ear. "I want you to step aside and let me have what is mine. If not...well," she straightened and smiled, "then you'll find other gifts besides a doll and a darling cat on your doorstep, maybe something three feet tall with curly hair." With a flip of her hair, she whirled and stalked away.

Coming toward us at a fast pace was Matt and Maryann. Rachel stopped, grabbed Matt's face in her hands, and landed a kiss on his lips that looked hot enough to rival the sun.

Still, it was nothing compared to the heat rising in my face as I struggled to keep my composure and focus on the next customer. The woman had a lot of nerve coming here and threatening me. If it was war she wanted, it was war she would get.

I forced another smile on my lips and signed a book for a lovely woman named Allison, while Matt forcefully extracted himself from Rachel's clutches before grabbing her arm and dragging her from the store.

I no longer had to pretend to smile. I had recognized the look on my fiance's face and tried not to gloat over the hot water Rachel had just landed in. Oh, to be able to eavesdrop on their conversation. That would be the highlight of my day.

By the time I'd signed three more books, Matt had returned, jaw clenched, and took up his stance next to my table. The customers cast him wary looks.

"Don't mind him," I said. "He's a disgruntled bodyguard."

"At least he's handsome," an elderly woman said. "He could guard me anytime, smiling or not."

I laughed. "There is that."

Other than a twitch of his lips, Matt pretended not to hear us. He stayed in that position for the next hour of my signing. By the time the last customer had left, I'd signed fifty books and taken orders for many more. I stood and popped the kinks from my back.

"Okay, handsome bodyguard, come over here and tell me what happened with Rachel."

"She's delusional. She must have been smoking too much loco weed on one of her travels."

"But, what did she say?" I tossed my empty paper coffee cup in a nearby trash can.

He exhaled sharply. "Here is not the place."

My blood chilled and I faced him. "I think here is exactly the place." While no one paid us any attention, whatever bad news Matt had to tell me was better said where I could not make a scene.

"She has a little girl."

My heart stopped.

"She says the child is mine."

I collapsed into my chair. "Is it possible?"

He shrugged. "It's possible. The child is three. I told Rachel I'd have to get a paternity test." He knelt in front of me. "This changes nothing, Stormi. I love you. If the child is mine, I'll take responsibility, but I'm going to marry you."

"I've never asked a lot of questions about your past." I sniffed back tears. "Maybe I should have."

"Do you love me?" The look in his eyes almost made me lose my strength and let the tears fall.

"With all my heart."

"Do you trust me?"

"With every fiber of my being."

He pulled me to my feet and into his arms. "Then nothing changes between us."

He was right. Rachel was probably lying. "Take me home?"

"Yes. I'll tell Maryann I'm riding with you." He gave me a quick kiss and darted off to find his sister.

A laugh from behind a display of new releases drew my attention. I turned and faced Rachel, my hands curling into fists.

"I can tell from the look of devastation on your face that Matt told you our good news."

"Go away before I shoot you." I reached for my purse.

"Tsk tsk." She crossed her arms. "I can see the headlines now, Best-Selling Author Murders Customer Inside Book Store."

"If your daughter is Matt's, then why wait until now to tell him?" I plopped my purse on the table. The gun inside made a satisfying clunk.

Rachel eyed the purse. "Why not? I never thought he was the marrying kind. There seemed to be all the time in the world to give him the news."

"Fooled you." I stood and slung my purse over my shoulder. "Matt will be back any second. I suggest you leave before he sees you. Oh, and Rachel?"

She raised her eyebrows.

"Mind yourself. Matt is a very good detective. If you aren't squeaky clean, and your daughter *is* his…well, you might find yourself with only visitation rights." I grinned and sashayed away, my roses cradled in my arms, leaving her with her mouth hanging open.

I wasn't normally a spiteful person, but that woman pulled the worst behavior out of me. I found Matt at the front of the store. From the shocked look on Maryann's face, he'd just broken the news to her.

She turned a wide-eyed look on me. "Are you all right?"

"Never better." I slipped my hand in Matt's. "Ready?"

"Yes." A look of relief crossed his features.

"No worries, Matt. It will all work out."

"I don't deserve you," he said.

"No one does." I winked at Maryann and led my man to the car. "You drive." I released his hand and dug the keys from my purse. "I'm going to sit here and finally get to enjoy my roses."

Once we were headed north on Interstate 40, I glanced at Matt. "That was the most interesting book signing I've ever had."

"I'm really sorry, Stormi. I've made

some mistakes in my life, but I never thought I'd have one like that come back to bite me…us." He reached over and grabbed my hand.

"It's fine. Really. We'll get through this. If you're a daddy, well, then, I'm a stepmother." I chuckled. "I threatened Rachel with removal of the child and you gaining custody if she didn't shape up."

"You what?" His eyes widened.

"I know it was petty, but it felt good at the time."

"You are full of surprises."

"So are you." I grinned and gave his hand a squeeze, then settled back in my seat for the hour drive home.

Rachel's news might have taken me by surprise, shocked me to my core, rocked my world, but I was strong. The love between Matt and me wasn't something a spiteful woman could easily destroy. Child or not, we'd be just fine.

Somewhere along the drive, I fell asleep. The next thing I knew we were pulling up in front of my house and Matt was shaking me awake. "It doesn't look as if your nephew went to school today."

I glanced at the front porch and groaned. Dakota sat on the swing, laptop in his lap. "He's taking the death of Mr. Dixon very hard. Seems to think he needs to spend all of his time hacking into the man's computer system."

"School is more important at his age." Matt exited the car and came around to open my door. "Do you want me to talk to him?"

"Would you? I've already tried. He fancies himself my tech guy, even wants a salary, and won't listen to the fact I said to go to school."

"Why don't you put those flowers away and I'll talk to him. Detective to delinquent boy."

He helped me from the car.

"Nice." I gave Dakota a stern look on my way inside and headed for the kitchen.

On the counter sat the remains of Mom's famous chocolate cake. Having missed dessert the night before because of snooping, I cut Matt and I a slice, poured two glasses of milk, and sat down to wait.

I didn't have to wait long. A contrite Dakota and his soon-to-be uncle joined me.

"He won't be missing school in the future," Matt said. "Go ahead and cut him a slice of that cake."

I nodded and slid Dakota my slice, then got up and cut myself another. "I'm glad to hear it."

"It isn't fair, but I don't want to have to go to court for truancy or have my Mom find out." Dakota dug into the cake. "But," he pointed his fork at me, "the things I'm finding out. Once you show me the list of his clients, I'll be able to solve this case."

"What list?" Matt glanced at me. "The one Wayne had you turn over to him? How many copies did you make?"

"One question at a time, please." I took my time getting my cake and milk. "Yes, those copies. I knew he would know I'd made a copy, so I made two and Maryann hid them in her shirt. I have no intentions of giving them to Dakota."

"There are some very influential names on that list, Stormi." Matt shook his head. "Names that will go to great lengths to keep their secrets."

"Even kill?"
He sighed. "Yes, even kill."

9

After a restless night's sleep, I sat in front of my laptop and searched the names on Dixon's client list. There were several influential business owners, some suburban housewives, even a local celebrity or two. Which of them would kill to keep Dixon quiet?

I tossed the papers on the desk next to my computer. After Rachel's bombshell the day before, concentration was in short supply. Much like my sleep the night before.

I smiled as Midnight grabbed Sadie's tail and wrapped his body around it. Sadie looked up at me with big brown eyes. I scratched behind her ears. "It's okay, girl. He won't hurt you."

Wait a minute. I grabbed the sheets of names and dashed to the foyer. Grabbing my purse, I shoved the papers inside, set the front door alarm, and rushed to my car. If anyone knew anything about these names, it might be Norma. After all, her clientele might once have been some of these very people.

When I arrived at the coffee shop, Tyler waved me back to Norma's office. I knocked, then entered at her invitation.

"Why don't you sit out there anymore?" I asked, sitting across from her.

"I hate accounting. Unless numbers are going into my bank account, I have no use for them." She closed her laptop. "I'm going to hire an accountant. I've been too cheap to fork out the expense, but if I don't want to pull my hair out, it's time. I don't want my customers to see me in a foul mood. What's up?"

I explained about finding the papers at Dixon's house and slid them across to her. "I'm hoping you might know some of these people."

"A prostitute doesn't…you

know…and tell." She wiggled her eyebrows.

"You aren't a prostitute anymore. Besides, weren't you more of a high-class call girl?"

"Semantics." She perched a cute pair of red-wire frame glasses on her nose and studied the pages. "Yes, I know several of these people. I think you can discount the wives spying on cheating husbands. I'd focus on these names." She took a pencil and checked off a few. "If anyone is capable of murder, these have the most to lose if they were doing something dirty."

"Thanks." I took the pages back as Tyler brought me my usual frozen mocha concoction. "I'm thinking of telling them that as a PI, Dixon was asking me to join his organization. Now that he's dead, I'll be taking over."

"You do like to walk a dangerous line." She shook her head. "I wish you'd give this up and focus on your writing. Hey." She grinned. "I've started writing a book. Now that our local erotica writer has left town, someone needs to take up the pen, so to speak. I'm taking your cue of writing about real-life events. Namely…my former profession. I'll change the names, of course."

"Now, who's walking dangerously? Some of the same people in your book are on my list."

"True, but you aren't changing names, and I'm not coming face-to-face with them."

I changed tactics and told her about Rachel. "I've put on a smile, but I'm not feeling happy about it at all."

"I don't blame you. That's a knock to the head for sure."

"It'll all work out. I love Matt enough to deal with whatever comes." I stood. "Thanks for your help. Let me take a look at your book when it's finished. If it's any good, I'll send it to my agent. But," I gave her a stern look, "I'll be brutally honest."

"That's how I want you to be." She grinned. "Go interrogate and leave me to the torture of accounting."

"Have fun." I closed the door after me and headed outside.

I stood on the sidewalk and contemplated turning over the new information to Matt and Wayne, but experience had taught me people were more likely to talk to me than the police. What I needed now was a plan of attack. Maybe Greta could help. She was an ex-cop. Surely, she had tips I could use.

I glanced both ways before crossing the street and caught sight of Mrs. Rogers, my neighbor and on again off again nemesis pointing a finger in Dakota's face. I sighed. Ditching school again. Maybe a trip to the High School would be my first plan of attack. I headed their way.

"What's up?" I crossed my arms and glared at my nephew.

"It's early release day," Dakota said.

I glanced at my watch. "At ten a.m.?"

"Your delinquent nephew is ditching." Mrs. Rogers scowled. "I watch all that goes on in our neighborhood and he's been missing a lot of school."

"Perhaps you would like to take over the Neighborhood Watch program. You're good at keeping tabs on everyone," I said.

"Maybe I will. You haven't done such a fine job keeping out the riff-raff."

"Because I don't have the help I

need." My next door neighbors, the Salazars, used to help me, but they've been on an extended vacation. Rusty, my simple-minded gardener, has also been out of the picture due to a family reunion in another state. "I'll start it back up if you'll sign up for one night a week. Unless roaming the streets at night frightens you."

"What scares me is what goes on in your den of inequity." She huffed and turned away. "I'll take Mondays and Wednesdays. Someone needs to take the initiative around here."

"As long as you don't start handing out a petition again to drive me and my family out of town, then you're welcome." I grabbed Dakota's arm, not trusting him to leave with the old woman. "We're heading to the station to talk with your mother."

"She's going to flip out."

"As she should."

I marched him to my car, then drove us to the station.

Angela scowled the moment we walked in the door. "Why is he out of school?"

"He's been ditching since Mr. Dixon died."

"I haven't gotten any alerts on my phone." She dug her cell phone out of her purse and checked for messages. "Nothing. Dakota?"

"I can't solve Mr. Dixon's death if I'm in some lame English class." Dakota crossed his arms, his look belligerent.

"I was wondering if you could get off work for an hour or so and come with me to the school," I said. "Maybe if we make a united front—"

"Since there's no man in the picture? That's what you mean, right?" Angela dropped her phone in her purse.

"I didn't say that. I thought you wanted my help." Sometimes she did, and at other times, I got the attitude.

She sighed. "I'll take an early lunch. Let me tell Wayne." She clomped down the hallway on four-inch heels.

"When did you become such a stick in the mud?" Dakota glared at me.

"Only when it's important. Like school."

Clomping heels signaled Angela's

return. I'd never understand how walking like a cow could be considered sexy, but since she was never without a boyfriend, I had to be missing something.

I slid into the driver's seat of my car, Angela taking the passenger side and Dakota got in the back. I turned the key in the ignition and thrust the car into reverse before glancing into my rearview mirror.

A face loomed.

I screamed.

"Rusty home!" He banged on the trunk and stalked away.

I rolled down my window. "That is not the way to announce yourself. I could have killed you." With my heart in my throat, I backed out and headed for the school.

When we arrived, I asked Dakota to step out of the car before turning to Angela. "Lance Miller, the principal, is on my list of suspects. I need you to flirt with him and make him comfortable." I eyed her exposed cleavage. "Bend over a few times."

"This is the real reason you offered to come."

"No, just one of the reasons." I grinned and shoved open my door.

Mother and son wore matching expressions of doom and gloom as we entered the administration office of the high school. I approached the counter. "We'd like to see Mr. Miller, please."

The secretary glanced at the clock. "Let me see if he's free. School releases in an hour, you know?"

I didn't, but I hoped our meeting wouldn't take that long. "Thank you."

We sat for a few minutes before a man in his early forties approached us with hand held out and a broad grin on his face. "I'm Mr. Miller. How may I help you?"

"Could we step into your office, please?" I asked. No sense in broadcasting our personal business all over town.

"Certainly. This way, please." He led us down a short hall and into an office with a large wood desk. Two chairs were placed before the desk and another two around a small table in the corner. "Sit there, son." He waved Dakota toward the table.

With a sharp glance at me, Angela turned her charm on the principal. She leaned forward, just a tad, and fluttered her false eyelashes. "I'm wondering why I haven't been informed about my son missing the last few days of school."

"I'm sorry to hear that. We're usually very good at keeping parents alerted to their student's behavior. What's your son's name?"

"Dakota Nelson." She smiled from under her lashes.

I wanted to gag, but I could tell her act was working. The man's attention was completely on her bosom, giving me the opportunity to study his office.

On a credenza against the wall were several framed photographs of Mr. Miller with a smiling brunette and two children of elementary school age. So, the man was married. Hmmm. I couldn't help but wonder how long ago he'd visited Norma, and why he was now a client of Dixon's. Or had Norma meant his wife was the client and Miller the one who would kill to keep things quiet?

"What is your phone number Mrs.

Nelson?" Miller grinned.

"Oh, it's Miss," Angela giggled. "Plenty of people make that mistake."

"Considering you don't look old enough to be this boy's mother, I can totally see that."

Angela giggled again and gave him her number.

I rolled my eyes and tried not to gag at the over-zealous flirtation of a married man.

"Well, I see the problem now. We have a different number for you." He rattled off a very familiar phone number.

I punched it into my phone. From where Dakota sat, we heard the theme song to Jurassic Park. One mystery solved.

Angela shot him a sharp look. "I take my child's education very seriously, Mr. Miller. What type of discipline do you enforce in situations like this?"

"After school detention for five days or two all day Saturdays. Which would you prefer?" Mr. Miller was suddenly all business. Most likely in a vain attempt to impress my sister.

She stuck her manicured pinkie in her mouth. "I think the Saturdays should suffice."

"Mom! I have things to do with my off time." Dakota lunged to his feet. "I have to help Aunt Stormi!"

"I guess that will have to be confined to the evenings." She stood and held out her hand to Mr. Miller. "Thank you for your time, but I must return to work. Dakota will finish out the short amount of the school day he has left."

"One moment, please." I stopped Miller as he made a move to walk my sister out. I handed him one of my business cards. "As a client of Mr. Dixon's, who is sadly no longer with us, I want to give you the opportunity to enlist my services." I grinned. "I now have his files and will be taking over his business."

Mr. Miller paled.

10

"You have *all* his files?"

Miller's words stopped me in the doorway. I turned and smiled. "Yes. He gave me all his files and recordings. Let me know if I can help you with anything." Feeling quite proud of myself, I sailed out the door and joined my sister in the reception area. Obviously, I missed Dakota slinking off to class.

"Did you get what you came for?" Angela asked, smiling at Miller who peered around the corner of the wall.

"Yep." I pushed open the front doors. Now to find a reason to visit the other two prime suspects on my list. Hank Caldwell, owner of Caldwell Construction could be hired for a project, maybe, but I had no reason to visit Susan Burnett, our ex-mayor's wife.

After dropping Angela back at work, I sat in my car, engine idling, and pondered my next move. Someone rapped on my window.

I shrieked and shrank back.

Miller stared in at me for a second before running around to the passenger side and hopping in. "I knocked first so you wouldn't shoot me."

"It was still a dumb move." I glared. "What do you want?"

He shut the door and turned sideways in his seat. "Do you really have Dixon's files?"

"What part of our conversation did you not understand?" And this man was responsible for the town's youths?

He licked his lips and exhaled sharply. "There are...certain...things, I don't need the town to know."

"Like, the fact a married man enjoys the company of prostitutes? I won't say a word." Eeew, the man grew slimier by the minute. "Or the fact you keep a mistress? Which one of those is a secret?"

He shrugged. "I have needs my wife can't fill. While I love her dearly, and would hate for her to find this out about me, it's something I must do."

"How far will you go to keep your secrets, Mr. Miller?" I casually slid my hand into my purse, reassured by the touch of my Tazor.

"I'm not sure I know what you mean." He frowned.

Maybe he really was as dense as he seemed. "Why are you here? You didn't really leave school to question a conversation we already had, did you?"

He seemed to think for a minute, then nodded. "I just wanted the reassurance that you can be trusted."

"I'm a licensed Private Investigator, bonded by the state, Mr. Miller."

"But...you write those books. My wife is a huge fan by the way."

"I change the names in my books." I'd also be taking a signed copy to Mrs. Miller. Perhaps she was a bit brighter than her husband. "You can get out of my car now."

He did, then leaned inside for one last remark. "I sincerely hope you are honest with your assurances. I'd hate for the same thing to happen to a pretty lady like you that happened to Dixon." He slammed the door and stormed to a black SUV parked behind me.

So, the threats begin. The only good thing about them is that threats signify I'm on the right track. I headed for the bakery to get Greta to use her skills in finding me Miller's home address. A chocolate cupcake wouldn't hurt either.

"Good afternoon," I said, entering the bakery.

Mom and Greta smiled at me from the other side of the counter.

"What do you need today?" Mom opened the display case. "I just made a fresh batch of red velvet cupcakes with cream cheese frosting."

"Sounds perfect." I swung open the waist-high saloon doors that kept customers from entering the back and took the delectable treat. "Greta, could you use your resources to get me an address for Lance Miller, the high school principal?"

"Sure? Mind sharing why?" She rolled her stool over to the computer.

I explained my visit to Norma as I ate. "If you have any bright ideas for meeting the other two at the top of the list, I'm all ears."

"Susan Burnett is head of the local beautifying committee," Greta said as her fingers flew across the keyboard. "You could always visit her on the pretense of making your yard look better."

My hand froze halfway to my mouth. "Is my yard ugly?" I thought Rusty did a good job.

"You could try planting some flowers come spring."

I shrugged and shoved the last of my treat into my mouth. "I suppose it's as good a reason to pick her brain as any. What about Caldwell? I don't really have any construction projects that need doing."

"You could finish the bathroom in the basement," Mom said. While she'd chosen the basement as her apartment under my house, it only had a toilet and a pedestal sink. "A bathroom in the attic for your sister would be nice, too."

"I guess I'm just made of money." I wasn't too sure I

wanted to hire a potential killer to do any renovations.

"Oh, hush." Mom tapped me on the head with a drying cloth. "You have plenty of money. Besides, what did you buy an old house for if not to fix it up?"

"I didn't expect to have the whole family move in with me." Now, that they had, I didn't want to change a thing. Until Matt I got married. Then, I might have to make some changes.

"Here's the address." Greta handed me a slip of paper. "Do you want me to put it in your GPS? I learned how the other day."

I grinned. "I can handle it, but thanks." I slipped off the stool I'd perched on. "Flowers, huh? Well, I guess Rusty can handle those along with the lawn and bushes."

"You might have to pay him more than ten dollars." Mom laughed.

I actually paid him eighty dollars to be my gardener, but he was stuck on ten because it's a larger number than eight. "I'll think of something." I gave her and Greta a hug and moved back to my car.

I must have slept wrong the night before because my lower back was starting to burn. It wouldn't hurt to take a nap before Matt came over for dinner. Speaking of…I had no idea what I was cooking. Since I hadn't spent time filling the freezer since we got back from New Orleans, I didn't have anything to thaw.

Wonderful. So much for a nap. I started the car and headed home.

My cell phone rang. It was the venue I'd chosen for my wedding reception, saying that they accidentally overbooked and could I choose another day? Really? Because it made sense to redo invitations and mail them out again. I told them no, and mentally added finding another venue at a late date to my to-do list. Matt and I should have eloped.

Back at the house, I set some steaks on the top of the fridge to thaw where Sadie couldn't reach them and headed for my office to find another venue. The Victorian garden and gazebo would have been perfect.

As luck would have it, I was able to find a venue by the lake. The white gazebo with party lights and autumn trees looked just as pretty as my first choice. A quick phone call later, I had a new venue that cost a few hundred more dollars. I sat back and stared at the picture on the website. Maybe…I wouldn't have the ceremony at the church. Getting married at sunset in that gazebo would be beautiful. I sent Matt a text, asking him if he was set on a church wedding.

He replied: As long as I'm marrying you, I'd get married in the middle of a dirt road.

Oh, how I loved that man.

I fished a bottle of Ibuprofen from my desk drawer and swallowed them with stale water from a bottle left on my desk. Hopefully, my back would get better fast.

In the kitchen, I tossed the empty bottle in the recycling bin and opened the refrigerator to check the items for a salad. Bless you, Mom, for going grocery shopping. I pulled out the needed ingredients, groaning as I straightened. What in the world was wrong with my back?

I spent the next half an hour preparing the salad and rooting in the cellar for the biggest potatoes we had. Steak, salad, and baked potatoes. What man wouldn't be happy with that?

If felt as if something jabbed me in the back. I groaned and leaned against the counter. I really did need to lie down on the heating pad for a few minutes.

Sadie raced past me, barking as if the hounds of hell were right outside the kitchen door. She placed her front paws against the window.

"Hush, girl." I swiped a hand across my sweating

forehead.

Her barks continued. I shuffled to the door and opened it. Well, one of hell's demons *was* there, actually.

Rachel stood, another stupid doll in her hand, holding a lit lighter to the doll's back. When she spotted me, she dropped the doll and the lighter and raced off, laughing.

I darted out the door and down the steps to take chase until she disappeared in the forest behind the house. The last thing I wanted to do was let some deranged jilted woman lure me into the woods. I glanced at my watch.

Just enough time to lie down for an hour before everyone came home. "Come on, Sadie." I tossed the burnt doll into the trash can and locked the kitchen door behind me. Seconds later, I climbed in bed and fell asleep.

"What is this?" Mom woke me, shaking the doll I'd thrown in the garbage in my face. "Did you get another one?"

I rubbed my eyes. "I caught Rachel in the backyard with it. Go away."

"It's time to get up and cook." She pulled the blankets aside. "Are you sick?"

I lay there for a moment. "No, I feel fine." No backache or headache. All I'd needed was a bit of sleep. "Is Matt here?"

"He's firing up the grill."

"Good." I grabbed the doll out of Mom's hands and marched down the stairs and outside. "Rachel left me another present. Can I punch her in the throat?"

He laughed and pulled me close with one arm. In the other, he held a spatula. "Only if I can watch." He bent down and kissed me. "Put a restraining order on her in the morning."

All was once again right with my world.

11

While I didn't hold much stock in restraining orders, I visited the police department and had one drawn up for Rachel. If she wanted to get close to me, a piece of paper wasn't going to stop her. Another good night's sleep and my back was as good as new.

I waited for Angela to put me in the system and checked my text messages. Norma sent me another suspect. Doctor Amanda Pritchard, famous plastic surgeon, known for her not so discreet infidelities. I didn't want to ask how Norma might know her, although I've suspected for a while that her ample bosom might not be the one God gave her.

"You ought to buy a charm," Angela said, handing me a copy of the order. "It would probably work better than this."

"Again, I don't believe in that stuff. See you later." I folded the paper and put it in my purse which still held the giant cross necklace. It was all the charm I needed. I was picking Maryann up from the coffee shop with our morning fuel, then on to see Mrs. Miller.

I pulled into a parking spot and left the car running while she got in, handing me my drink. "You got Norma's text?" she asked.

"Did she say why the woman was a suspect?"

Maryann shook her head. "Only that she'd heard things."

It might the hardest excuse yet to come up to see her since I had no desire for plastic surgery of any kind. I supposed I could use the same ruse I used on Lance Miller; that I was taking over Dixon's business.

As we drove, I told Maryann about switching wedding venues and my desire to have the wedding ceremony in the same location as the reception. "It'll be beautiful and no one will have to drive somewhere else."

"I think it's perfect. Will they let us decorate the day before?"

I cut her a sideways glance. "I didn't ask. I guess I should have."

"I'll take care of it. As your maid-of-honor, it's one of my jobs."

I laughed. "You have a lot of jobs on my behalf."

"Good thing you pay well."

We talked about wedding details until I turned down a street of modest ranch-style homes. Checking the houses on each side, I found the one the Millers owned and turned into the driveway.

Maryann handed me a copy of my first book, I signed it, and we exited the car. I didn't have a clue how to bring up her husband hiring Dixon, and prayed the opportunity to mention it would arise.

As we marched to the front door, I took note of the fall foliage in large barrels on each side of the porch. Not only were they overflowing with mums and greenery, but reflector balls caught the sun's rays. Along each side of the house were climbing rose bushes that must be beautiful in the spring. Maybe we could talk about flowers to break the ice.

I lifted the metal rapper on an ornate doorknocker and waited.

The door opened two inches. "If you're soliciting, we don't want any."

"We're not here to sell you anything." I stepped to where she could see me better. "I'm—"

"Glory be, you're Stormi Nelson." The door opened all the way. A short, slightly overweight woman in expensive jeans and beaded top beamed up at me. She looked to be about my age, but the whiskey wafting off her was aging her quickly. She also wasn't the woman in the photo on Miller's desk. "What in the world brings you to my house?"

I smiled, prepared to continue the ruse the woman and Miller obviously had going. "I had the opportunity to speak with your husband yesterday and he mentioned you were a fan. Since I'm out running errands, I thought I'd bring you a signed copy." I held out the book.

"Wonderful. Come in." She stepped aside, ushering us in, while muttering very unflattering things under her breath about her husband.

I glanced at Maryann, who shrugged.

"I've just put on some coffee and baked a cake this morning. Please, sit, and enjoy some with me." She left us in a floral-decorated living room and bustled out of sight.

I perched on a chintz sofa covered in plastic, wincing at the crackling sound as I sat. Doilies covered the arms of the sofa and two easy chairs. A crocheted table runner ran the length of the coffee table. If I didn't know better, I'd think I was sitting in my grandmother's living room, rather than a woman's around my own age.

"It's a good thing I'm wearing pants," Maryann said, "or my legs would stick to the plastic."

"If something happened to you, there'd at least be DNA from the skin left behind." I grinned, shifting to try and get comfortable.

"My apologies," Mrs. Miller said. "My husband inherited this house years ago when his mother passed and refuses to let me change a thing. If not for my flowers, I'd go insane."

Her flowers and her alcohol. A bottle of Kahlua sat in

the middle of the coffee tray. She picked up the bottle. "Cream?"

I shook my head. "No, thank you."

Maryann's eyes widened. "Just sugar, please."

"Suit yourselves, goody-two-shoes." She poured an ample amount of the drink into her coffee, then turned back with a smile. "I heard somewhere that you were also a private investigator, Stormi. Is that true?"

"Yes, ma'am." I took a sip of the most bitter coffee I'd had in a long time. I thought longingly of my mocha sensation in the car.

"Well, I don't cotton to snooping, but my husband needs to be followed. I'd like to hire you. I hired that Dixon fellow, but he went and got himself killed. Carelessness." She took a gulp of her coffee and closed her eyes. A look of pleasure crossed her face.

"What makes you think he needs spying on?" I pretended to drink.

"I forgot the cake!" She set her cup down, leaped to her feet and then rushed to the kitchen. She returned a few minutes later with thick slices of cinnamon bread on three plates. "Sometimes, I'd lose my head if it weren't attached."

I thought her forgetfulness might have something to do with the alcohol, but wisely held my tongue. "You were saying."

"I really do appreciate you bringing me this book." She caressed the cover. "I'll treasure it always."

"You were going to hire me—"

"Right. To follow my no-account, cheating husband." She took another drink of her coffee. "What ridiculous amount do you charge? Dixon took a hundred dollars an hour. I gave him all the information he needed, too. All he had to do was take a few pictures. Instead, he got himself killed."

"You don't know whether he took any photographs?"

"If I did, I wouldn't need you." She narrowed her eyes. "Did I thank you for the book?"

I nodded.

She dug in her bosom and brought out a folded hundred dollar bill. "I'll pay you the same." She thrust it at me.

Gross. "Why do you think your husband is cheating, Mrs. Miller?"

"Everyone knows that, sweetie. He's been chasing the skirt of that secretary of his for years. I just ain't caught him." Another swig of her coffee. "But you…you'll catch him. You catch all them killers." She cackled, then froze. "Are you looking for Dixon's killer? The no-account thief."

I decided to keep that information to myself. "I'm just here to drop off the book."

"And take my case. Don't forget that." She set her coffee cup on top of the book I gave her.

I stifled a gasp. Did she have no respect?

"Eat." She waved at the cake. "It ain't poisoned. You writers are always thinking the worst. It's because you have an overactive imagination." As if she'd just noticed Maryann, she transferred her attention like a bat spotting a bug. "What's your role in all this?"

Maryann swallowed the bite of the cake she'd taken. "I'm Stormi's assistant."

"Yes. You do her dirty work, poor thing. You need some cream." She poured a healthy dose of Kahlua into Maryann's coffee."

Since Maryann hadn't keeled over dead from the cake, I took a bite. It was amazing. Sugar and cinnamon swirled together in a moist cake. "Delicious!"

"My mother-in-law's recipe, God rest her soul." Mrs. Miller stood again. "I guess you'd better be going. You have a lot of work to do. Give me a call if you find out anything."

She scribbled her phone number on the back of an electric bill from a side table. "Ooops. I bet you don't want to be paying my bills." She opened the envelope, withdrew the contents, and handed me the outside. "I want some photos."

I was pretty sure I knew where to find some, too. If Dixon had taken any, they would be on the files Dakota was trudging through. "I'll find out for you. It was nice to meet you. Thank you for the cake and coffee. Oh, and it isn't good for the book to use it as a coaster."

"It's mine to do as I want." She slammed the door behind us as we stepped onto the porch.

"That was the strangest visit I've ever had," Maryann said.

"That woman is not his wife, but she thinks she is." I cast a look behind us in time to see the curtains twitch. Yep, a strange woman, that one. "Why fool around on the respectable-looking, attractive woman I saw in a photo in his office?"

She shrugged. "Now what?" Maryann asked when we were in the car.

"We head home and see what's on the files Dakota brought over. If Dixon had something on Miller, then we have it now." I eyed my melted coffee drink. Deciding it had to still be better than what Mrs. Miller served us, I took a big sip. Yep, better.

Back at the house, I headed upstairs and sat in Dakota's office chair while Maryann perched on his unmade bed. I scanned file after file and got nowhere. Dixon had the strangest filing system I'd ever seen.

I turned to Maryann. "Did you see a camera in Dixon's house anywhere?"

"No, but he was bound to have one. If so, the police have it now."

"They didn't know about the hole in the floor. Maybe

they didn't find it."

"Or…" she grabbed her cell phone from her pocket and punched in some numbers. "Yes, this is Nelson Investigations, and we're looking into Mr. Dixon's personal effects. Did he, by chance, leave anything with you to be developed? He did? Wonderful. We'll be right over." She hung up and grinned. "Digital age or not, he would still need quality photos to be printed. That printer he had in his office was not photo quality."

"You are marvelous!"

We sped to the drugstore where Maryann repeated her spiel to the young girl behind the counter. The cashier then handed us a white cardboard envelope.

"Did you look at them?" I asked.

"I had to. I developed them. But, I'm also sworn to secrecy." She shuddered. "There's a lot of filth living in this town."

I agreed. "Thank you." We headed back to the car. I opened the envelope and pulled out an inch thick pile of photos.

The few on top were of the lovely Doctor Pritchard in lacy underwear in a sleazy hotel. The next was of the mayor's wife stepping through the doors of the same hotel with a man I didn't recognize. Then, we feasted our eyes on a heavy set man paying for a lap dance at a bar. He must be Caldwell. Finally, the last five photos were of Lance Miller.

There wouldn't be anything wrong with the photos taken through a large plate glass window, except the woman and children he was eating dinner with were definitely not the woman we'd just met.

12

Maryann and I took the photos back to the house and spread them across the kitchen table. "What do we do with this information?" she asked.

"Probably hand it over to the police."

I turned to see Matt grinning from the doorway. I rushed into his arms and tilted my face for a kiss. "You know that isn't going to happen short of an official demand."

He obliged my want of a kiss. "I know. Show me what you have." He shook his head. "The things I let slide with you."

"Because you love me and know I always get my guy, or gal." I took his hand and led him to the table.

"Sometimes at great expense, but yes, you always catch the bad guy." He crossed his arms and stared at the photos while I filled him in on my conversation with Norma and everything else Maryann and I had done.

"The supposed Mrs. Miller is a few chips short of a Pringle's can," I said. "But, she did hire me to find out if her fantasy husband is cheating on her. What do I do with these photos? It looks as if the man has an entirely different family."

"More like half a can," Mom said, entering the kitchen and digging in a bottom cupboard. "I've known that woman since moving here. Cheryl Miller might be kooky, but she usually gets what she wants. There it is!" She pulled out a porcelain Dutch oven. "Greta wants to borrow this." She straightened. "See y'all at supper."

"I guess we visit these people." Matt watched Mom leave, then turned to me. "They've all become our top suspects in Dixon's murder. Stormi, you have wonderful instincts. What is your gut telling you?"

"Not much." I sat in a kitchen chair. "Other than these pictures, I don't have a lot of info to go on. Greta suggested I approach Susan Burnett about her gardening club, and I could see about getting a quote from Caldwell for renovations, but Amanda Pritchard is a mystery. I have no idea how to talk to her."

"I'll try to get a female officer from Little Rock to do some investigative work for us."

If anyone could convince a woman of anything, it was my Matt. "Why don't you visit her? All you'd have to do is turn on the charm." I grinned.

"I'm too beautiful as it is. She'd never buy me looking into plastic surgery." He winked and scooped up the photos. "I promise to make copies of these and give them back. We're too small of a police force to turn down the type of help you can give us. Just be careful."

"As always."

"Right." He planted a quick kiss on my lips, a peck on Maryann's cheek, and left.

"Good thing we have the negatives." Maryann waved the envelope in the air. "I recognize that look on my brother's face. He'll take his sweet time getting us those pics. It's to the one hour photo for us."

"You're a genius." I'd recognized the look, too, and was prepared to overdose my fiancé with my feminine wiles to get the photos back. I grabbed my keys and off we went again.

The young photo developer didn't bat an eyelash at our return. She merely shrugged and got to work. A well-palmed twenty dollar bill put our job ahead of others.

"Do we head back to Miller first thing?" Maryann asked. She held up a coffee mug. "I think I'll get one of these with mine and Michael's picture on it and give it to him. If he drinks out of my face every day, maybe he'll move our relationship along a little faster."

I flipped through the catalog the photo shop had displayed on their counter. I still didn't have party favors for the wedding guests. Maybe napkins with mine and Matt's engagement picture on them?

Speaking of…"I need a photographer fast for engagement photos."

"I'll take them." Maryann frowned. "I have a great Nikon camera. Save your money for a wedding photographer."

"Great. This afternoon, by the lake, at three o'clock." I texted Matt to show up wearing jeans and the blue button up I loved him in. I'd actually don a maxi-length sundress. I could brave the autumn temperatures for the sake of a picture. One more thing off my wedding to-do list. "But, we still need a photographer for the wedding."

"You really need to use the wedding planner book I gave you." Maryann gave me a look that clearly said I was doing things the hard way. "It takes you step-by-step. You're so far behind in some of the things you need to do, that it's scary."

"I have the dress and the groom. Everything else is extra." I paid the developer and took the envelope with the newly developed pictures.

"I didn't say anything last time," the girl said, "but that picture of Dr. Pritchard looks Photoshopped."

"Really?" I pulled out the photo.

"Look at the lighting." She pointed to where the man had a definite shadow from a table lamp. The doctor had none. "Not only that, but look at her head...see where the neck doesn't quite match up? This is only my opinion, but I think someone has it out for the doctor."

It was very clear now that she pointed it out. "Thank you." I wasn't yet sure what I would do with the information, but it did give me a reason to visit the plastic surgeon. As a private investigator, of course.

Next, Maryann and I stopped for a fast food burger, eating it on the way to Cheryl Miller's. I couldn't quite call it Lance Miller's anymore. It was quite clear the man preferred to be somewhere else. Not that I could blame him too much. Still, there were more moral, and lawful, ways of getting out of a fake marriage.

We pulled in front of the house. Cheryl had clearly not stopped drinking and now swayed with a water hose, missing her plants more than she watered them. "Hellooooo." She waved her fingers. "Fancy seeing you so soon."

I took a deep breath and opened the car door. "We have what you asked for." I grabbed only the photos of her husband, leaving one behind for my use.

She turned and soaked my shoes. "Ooops." She bent and turned off the water.

Groaning, I handed her the photos, while Maryann stood a safe foot behind me and to the side. What was she afraid of? I'd already checked and other than the water hose, I didn't see any weapons close at hand.

Cheryl studied the photos, then dropped them on the ground and stomped on them. "I suspected something like this. The man is never home!" She cursed then grabbed the water hose and soaked the photos. "I want to know who the woman is."

"I don't think that's wise. The best thing to do would be to file for divorce on the grounds of infidelity."

She laughed. "We aren't married, sweetie. I'm the other woman. We just happen to have the same last name." She bent over and pounded her leg, still laughing. "That rat told me he left his wife years ago and was going to marry me. What a lying cheater."

That was a bit of the pot calling the kettle black, but I let it go.

"Here I am, waiting on that fool, at his beck and call, bored out of my mind." She straightened, all traces of laughter gone. "Do you know how long it's been since he's visited? Six months!"

Again, I held my tongue as to why I thought he stayed away. "Have you thought of moving on?"

Before I could blink, her nose was an inch from my face. "Look at me! Look what waiting on him has done to me. I used to be beautiful. What man wants this?" She whirled and stormed into the house, slamming the door.

"You didn't get paid," Maryann said in a small voice.

"I'd rather not." I glanced at the soggy, wrinkled photos, then headed back to the car. I really wasn't in the mood to visit anyone else. Instead, I'd get ready for my afternoon photo session.

By three o'clock, feeling very pretty and a bit chilly in my summery dress, I waited by the lake for Matt. He'd texted that he was running fifteen minutes late. I sat on a bench next to Maryann and rubbed my arms for warmth.

A family skipped rocks across the lake's surface. The father turned, and I gasped. Lance Miller in broad daylight. For some reason, I'd thought he might have his family and mistress stashed in separate towns, but I guess not.

He caught me staring and turned away. The louse probably thought Dixon had photos of him with Cheryl, other than the opposite. I contemplated about telling him, and decided a man like that deserved to stew for a while.

Oh, no. He'd obviously thought about it and decided to come talk.

I glanced at Maryann. "Keep a look out for Matt. I doubt this jerk will cause a scene with his family here, but you never know."

"Miss Nelson."

"Mr. Miller."

"Have you thought more of what we

discussed?"

I gave a wry smile. "I've thought on it a lot, and discovered you don't deserve that lovely family over there. But, for the sake of the children, I'll not say a word about your alcoholic mistress living a few miles away."

His face darkened. "Good. See that you don't."

"You aren't threatening my fiancé, are you, Lance?" Matt stood behind him, arms crossed, a stern look on his face.

"No, officer. Just making conversation." Miller returned to his family.

Matt's face softened as his gaze fell on me. "Ready to take some pictures of a couple in love?"

"More than ready." I stepped into his arms.

"Are you all right?"

"Perfect, now that you're here. Besides, I think he's all talk. He isn't going to jeopardize what he has. It's pretty obvious the only one who doesn't know the relationship is over is the mistress."

"Let's go before we lose the light,"

Maryann said. "Shop talk can wait."

"We don't want to upset my bossy little sister." With his arm around my shoulder, Matt led me to a tree displaying vibrant yellow leaves. The lake sparkled in the background.

We spent the next half hour goofing around and taking pictures. I couldn't think of a more perfect ending to the day.

After our photo shoot, we headed back to the house where I planned to make a big pot of spaghetti complete with cheesy garlic bread. After supper, Matt and I really needed to talk about where we were going to live after we were married.

By eight o'clock, we were nestled under a quilt on the front porch, laughing each time the Olson's curtains or Mrs. Rogers's twitched back into place when our audience grew tired of watching us do nothing more than talk.

"I'll live anywhere you want to, Stormi." Matt rested his chin on the top of my head.

"I really love this house. Do you think we'll regret the lack of privacy?"

"Probably, but I come from a small

family. I love the noise and bustle of yours. When you visit Caldwell, why don't you plan on moving Angela into the master bedroom and make a small apartment upstairs for us? A bedroom, bathroom, and a small sitting area. Then, when we need some quiet, we have a place to go."

"That's a wonderful idea. I can still enjoy the beauty of the house, but we'll have our honeymoon retreat."

I could only hope that Caldwell didn't turn out to be the killer. He was the closest construction company Oak Meadows had.

13

The next morning, I placed a call to Caldwell Construction, specifically asking that Hank Caldwell be the one who gives me the estimate. I was promised he would arrive within the hour.

Now, I stood in the attic, slash Angela's apartment, and envisioned the tirade when she found out she would have to share a room with Cherokee until the renovations were complete. They'd hear her screams in New York City. I'd had minor renovations done a few months ago, but if this was going to be mine and Matt's retreat, there was a lot more work to be done.

I shrugged. If she didn't like the accommodations, she could move.

Where was my mocha drink? Maryann promised to have it in my hand well before Caldwell arrived. I was sure I would need the fortitude before knowing how much the renovations were going to cost me. Still, I was happy that Matt was willing to live with my crazy family.

"I'm sorry." Maryann thundered up the attic stairs. "The contractor is here early and wandering around the outside of the house." She thrust my drink into my hand.

"Most likely chalking up additional things wrong with my house." I took a sip and rushed down the stairs and outside.

A burly man in his mid-to late fifties walked the perimeter of my house making notes on a clipboard while Sadie barked from the kitchen window. The man turned. "That dog will have to be locked up before we can start work."

"She isn't vicious. I'm Stormi Nelson, can I help you?"

He nodded. "Hank Caldwell. You asked for renovations. I've been making a list."

"I want the attic renovated, not the

rest of the house."

"Oh. My bad. Would you like to show me the area?"

I studied the three-day growth of beard on his square face, the beady eyes and slight paunch. Looks notwithstanding, I didn't think I liked the man. It was nothing more than a feeling, but I wasn't usually too far off the mark. I'd show him the attic, get some referrals, and let him know I had Dixon's files before actually signing on the dotted line. Maybe I'd have Matt meet him. I didn't want any shenanigans just because I was a woman. "Follow me."

I led him through the house, hiding a grin around the straw of my drink as he made a wide berth around a growling Sadie. It wasn't like my big furry girl to be so antagonistic. "She doesn't like you."

"Most dogs don't. It's weird."

Hmm. Dogs were usually a great judge of character. "Maryann, would you mind coming to the attic with us?" I poked my head into my office as we passed. I decided to trust my dog's instincts and not be alone with the man.

She joined us immediately and the three of us tromped up the stairs I'd had built when Angela moved in. "I want a nice handrail on these stairs," I said. "I want them to look as if they've always been here." In the attic, I led him around the mess and piles of clothes. "I want this to be basically a large, modern master suite. Large bathroom with separate jet tub and shower, two vanities, separate water closet—"

"What's that?" He looked up from his notes.

"The little room where you put the toilet."

"Oh." He wrote that down.

"A large walk in closet with space enough for a padded bench. I want the closet custom. I'll draw you up some designs." I planted my fists on my hips. "I've already had heating and cooling put in, so that's about it."

"This is going to be expensive." He glanced up from under bushy eyebrows.

"Oh, that's no bother. Since taking over Dixon's investigative services, and combined with my own, the money will be there." I crossed my arms and tilted my head, ready for his reaction. I wasn't disappointed.

His eyes narrowed. "What do you mean?"

"Why, right before Dixon was murdered," I drew out the word, "we agreed to go into business together. He gave me copies of all his files and recordings. Now that he's gone, I guess it's just me and my associates."

"Associates?" He paled.

"Yes. There are three of us. Oh," I put a finger to my lips, "you were one of Dixon's clients. I guess that means you are now mine. Do I get a discount on construction services?"

"Or what?"

"It's just a question."

"What do you plan on doing with the information Dixon handed to you?"

"Why, nothing. Not until the person who actually hired him wants me to. From your reaction, I gather that wasn't you. Of course, it wasn't. You wouldn't hire someone to take pictures of you at a strip club. How silly of me. Well," I rubbed my hands together, "that's about all here. How long until you get back to me? Oh, and I'd like some references on your work, please."

"Three days." He stomped down the stairs.

Sadie barked loud and shrill.

The front door slammed.

"That went well." I turned to Maryann.

"How so? We're adding to our suspect list rather than taking away."

"Once we've confronted everyone on the list Norma gave us, we can then start pushing people to make a move or to back away."

"You love to live dangerously." She shook her head. "Where to now?"

I chewed the inside of my bottom lip. "I could call about making an appointment with Doctor Pritchard." I know Matt was sending an undercover cop, but they didn't know about the Photo-shopped pictures. I wondered whether Dixon would have altered the photo, but couldn't think of a single reason why he would. Still, he had the photo on his negatives. Which meant...he had to have taken a picture of the photo. Why?

"Let's go see Matt." We headed to the car and then to the police station, Pritchard's photo in hand.

Once there, Matt led us to his office and studied the photo. "This doesn't make sense."

"A lot of things don't make sense." I sat in a chair across from his desk. "It looks suspiciously like blackmail to me."

Matt's phone rang. He hit the speaker button.

"Rachel Gable is demanding to see you." My sister's voice came through loud and clear.

Matt met my gaze. "Send her away."

"She won't leave."

"Then make her wait." He punched the button to hang up. "She's probably here about the restraining order."

"Good." I grinned. "Now, back to the task at hand." I refused to let that woman disrupt my life any more than she already had.

Angela rang again. "I'm sorry."

Rachel burst into Matt's office. She

got a smug look when she saw me. "Oh, good. The gang's all here." She handed Matt a sheet of paper. "When would you like to meet your daughter?"

Matt laid the paper on his desk. "So, the results came in. I'm a father." A muscle ticked in his jaw. "I don't have time to discuss this right now."

If she knew him as well as she said she did, Rachel would have turned and fled the room. Instead, she stepped around his desk and laid a hand on his arm. Stupid woman.

"Can't you see why you can't marry someone else?"

"Not at all. You kept the fact I had a daughter from me for three years, so it hasn't been a big concern to you." He gripped his arm and dragged her toward the door. "I suggest you leave or I'll have you thrown out."

"But—"

He pushed her into the hall and slammed his door. "I'm sorry about that." He turned red-rimmed eyes on me.

I rushed to his side. "We'll work through this."

He pulled me into his arms. His shudders tore through me. "I have a daughter I never knew about. I don't even know her name."

The door closed behind us. Maryann most likely left to respect our privacy.

Without speaking, Matt and I stood, slightly swaying, just holding each other. My heart raced out of fear. A child changed so many things in our life. I loved the little girl, despite her horrible mother, because Matt's blood ran in her veins. But, the thought of Rachel in our life for a very long time filled me with dread.

"Let's get married now. Today," Matt said. "We can still have the formal ceremony as planned, but—"

I pulled back. "No. Nothing will change between us. We won't get married because we're afraid of what that evil woman will do. Hey, at least now the childish voodoo games will stop." I gave him a shaky smile.

He gazed into my eyes. "I don't deserve you."

"Oh, I think we're made for each other." I rose on my toes and kissed him.

"Let's get back to work, shall we?"

He kissed me again, then again, as a man starving for a life-saving drink of water. He pulled back and rested his forehead against mine. "I'll pass the photo on to the undercover cop and pay a visit to Caldwell on the pretense of seeing his notes on the renovation. You keep on Miller and visit with Susan Burnett. Be careful."

"I will." I cupped his face. "Keep the faith. God is in this."

"I know. I'm sorry I'm not coming to you as pure as you are to me."

I chuckled. "One of us needs to know what they're doing." I turned and left, casting one last look over my shoulder.

Matt stood at his desk staring at the paternity test.

The fact Rachel held on to the fact he was a father made me more angry than her trying to break up our marriage. I recognize a desperate woman who knew she was losing the battle and almost felt sorry for her. I wasn't the type of person to break off a wedding to the man I loved because of something in his past. No matter how big.

I met up with Maryann in the waiting room.

"Is everything all right?" she asked.

"It's all going to be just fine." I approached Angela's desk. "You'll need to clear out the attic and move in with Cherokee for a few weeks. I'm renovating the attic into a space for me and Matt."

"What?! Of all the nerve—"

I held up a hand to ward off her screeching. "My house, my money, my wants. See you at supper." I turned and marched into the fall afternoon. I loved my sister, but sometimes she needed to be put in her place.

A brisk breeze had picked up. Leaves in autumn splendor rained upon the parked cars. The only thing marring the beauty of the day was the smug woman sitting on the hood of my car.

"Get off before you dent the hood," I told her, pressing the unlock button on my car fob. "Remember the restraining order."

"You'd have the mother of Matt's child arrested?"

"In a heartbeat." I grinned. "If you're behind bars, you're no longer a problem. Then, we could get the court to order a psych eval. Wouldn't that be interesting?"

She called me a few choice names as I got into the driver's seat, then kicked the front fender. I couldn't help but laugh out loud as she limped away.

"Things are never going to be the same," Maryann said. "I don't have a clue how to be an aunt."

"I don't have any idea how to be a stepmother." I turned the key in the ignition and backed out of the parking spot. "We'll figure it out."

"I bet Matt fights for custody. If he does, he'll win. That will make you a full time mother."

I took a deep breath. Attic renovations might change…again.

14

The ringing of my cell phone from my nightstand woke me the next morning. I fumbled for the phone, knocking it to the floor in the process, and upsetting three cats and one very large dog who had all somehow managed to sneak into bed with me.

I finally had the phone in hand, and hanging half on the bed and half on the floor, pushed the answer button. "Hello?"

"I'd like to speak with Stormi Nelson." A cultured, feminine voice said.

"This is she." I glanced at the clock. Eight a.m. I couldn't remember the last time I'd slept this late.

"This is Doctor Amanda Pritchard. I'd like to hire your services. Could you meet me at the quaint coffee shop in Oak Meadows at nine?"

"Oh. Yes. I'll be there."

The woman hung up and had me dashing for the shower, calling Maryann on my way. "Get over here within thirty minutes." I hung up and set my phone in the vicinity of the sink. A splash alerted me to the fact I'd missed and the ever-accommodating toilet caught the phone.

"No!" I plunged my hand into the bowl and retrieved my phone.

After a few seconds of whirling like a dervish, hoping for a miracle, I raced downstairs and to the kitchen for a bag of rice. I took the phone apart and buried the pieces deep into the rice. Zipping the bag closed, I took it with me back to my room and left it sitting safely on the bed under the watchful eye of my pets.

Forty minutes later, I shoved the bag of rice and phone into my purse and thundered downstairs. I'd made the point of wearing black slacks and a long-sleeved royal blue blouse. I'd slapped on some makeup and pinned my hair into a sloppy bun. I wanted to have a semblance of professionalism when meeting with someone of the doctor's caliber.

Maryann glanced up from the kitchen. "Must be important if you're out of jeans."

"Doc Pritchard called. We're meeting her in twenty minutes at Delicious Aroma."

She frowned. "You should have told me. I would have worn something other than a grey maxi skirt and sweatshirt."

"At least the sweatshirt has lace down the arms." Maryann would look nice in a feed sack.

We made it to the coffee shop at five minutes til nine. I hollered across the room for Tyler to make our usuals, then chose a round table set apart from the rest.

Norma sent a curious look our way, which was replaced with one of surprise when Pritchard walked into the room. Norma mouthed, "Wow," and pretended to concentrate on the laptop screen in front of her.

Pritchard must know who I am because she made a beeline to our table. "Miss Nelson?"

"Yes." I stood and offered my hand. "Please, have a seat and my assistant will get you something to drink."

Pritchard barely glanced at Maryann and said, "Black. Cream and sugar. The biggest they have."

Maryann rolled her eyes and hurried to the counter, bypassing the line, to the disgruntled murmurs of those waiting. I didn't blame her. I wouldn't want to miss a second of our meeting with the beautiful doctor either. Despite making an effort with my appearance, I felt shoddy and underdressed.

Amanda Pritchard, she said I could call her Amanda, which made me feel ridiculously privileged, set her Gucci bag on the table and twined her string of pearls around her fingers. "I'm a bit embarrassed to be here."

"I'm guessing you know that I've taken over for Dixon." I took my drink from Maryann.

"Yes, but I was never the one to hire him." She pursed her lips. "It seems as if someone is out to tarnish my reputation."

It wasn't that sparkly to begin with,

but okay. "Who would want to do that?"

She exhaled sharply. "My ex-husband, more than likely." She gave a sharp laugh. "He's a web designer for several major corporations and sticking my head on some slut's body would be an easy feat for him."

"So, you weren't in that motel with the mayor?" Oh, yeah. The man's identity had come to me while I was sleeping. The paling of her skin told me I hadn't dreamed the man's name.

"Former mayor, and no, I never had." She pulled harder on her pearls. "But...this isn't common knowledge, although a few people obviously are aware of the fact...I intend to run for mayor. I believe that is the reason for the photographs."

Also a very good motive on her part to knock off Dixon. "How did you find out I had the photos?"

She gave a tight-lipped smile. "Word gets around."

While we talked, Maryann took notes on her Ipad. She made the perfect assistant. Not many people could sit there quietly and blend into the background while someone spilled their motive for murder.

A tall man with a camera approached our table, snapped a quick photo, and skedaddled before we could say a word.

"Wonderful." Amanda stopped fiddling with her necklace. "Who knows what the paper will make of this little meeting." She stood and grabbed her purse. "Find out who is setting me up, Miss Nelson, and send the bill to my office." She sauntered from the coffee shop.

"Do you think she killed Dixon?" Maryann turned off her Ipad.

"She's as good a suspect as the others. I guess we'll find out if she threatens me in any way." I took a sip of my coffee, noticing Amanda hadn't touched hers. "My question is…does she know the undercover cop Matt sent is an undercover cop? I'm not sure it would matter at this point, but maybe hiring me is nothing more than a red herring."

"The only person on this list we haven't spoken to is Susan Burnett."

"Call and make us an appointment." I leaned back in my chair, putting all four legs back on the floor when Norma glared at me.

Maryann looked up Susan Burnett's phone number and placed the call. When she hung up, she smiled. "She was excited to hear you want to join her garden club and can see us now."

"Then, let's go." I waved at Norma, then headed back to the car. It sure seemed like I spent a lot of time in my Mercedes lately.

"Isn't that Dakota?" Maryann pointed to a young man ducking around the corner at the end of the street.

"Yep." I switched directions and went after my once again truant nephew.

We chased him down the alley, well, not as in ran, but as in followed. He darted between buildings, coming out across from the bank. He lifted a camera and snapped a photo as Hank Caldwell planted a kiss on Cheryl Miller. It looked as if the mistress had found herself another man…in record time, too.

When Dakota ducked back into the

alley, I grabbed his arm. "What are you doing?"

"Taking photos." He looked up at me as if to say 'duh'. "I took this camera from Mr. Dixon's shop. He'd always told me that it would be mine someday."

"It's still stealing until his estate is settled."

"Then, I'm borrowing it."

"Why aren't you in school?"

"Teacher development day." He put the lens cap on the camera. "Did you see those two across the street? Eew. Since you won't let me skip school," he looked as if that were cruel and unusual punishment, "I have to do what I can when I can. Want to see what I've uncovered?"

"Here or at the house?"

"The house."

"We're headed to Susan Burnett's. Can we meet you at home in an hour or so?"

He nodded. "I'll get these photos developed by then. You should really build me a dark room if I'm going to be your photographer." He raced away.

My IT guy *and* my photographer. Angela was going to kill me. She had her hopes on her son being a doctor or a lawyer, not working for her sister. I didn't plan on renewing my PI license indefinitely. What would Dakota do then?

I shrugged and walked back to the car with Maryann. This time, we had no diversions and soon found ourselves in front of a two-story, plantation style house on the outskirts of town. It might not be the mayor's mansion, but it was close. "Does being the mayor pay this well?"

"Susan's family has money," Maryann said. "It's rumored that that's why Lincoln married her. They've been in this town since its beginning. They used to be an upstanding family. Susan is all that is left of the Sharps."

"I love how full of information you are."

"I'm a nerd." She grinned. "I love to read the town's history and gossip columns."

"I'm glad you're a nerd." I redid my bun, brushed some dust from my pants, and exited the car.

The Burnett home had a crushed shell walk up to the house and a lion's head doorknocker. To the right was a button. I pushed it and listened as Winchester chimes rang out. While I waited for someone to answer the door, I surveyed the yard beyond the curving driveway.

Sculpted bushes, trailing ivy, and oaks sporting their autumn splendor proved that any garden Susan might have would be something to see indeed. I couldn't wait to get a load of it come spring.

A woman in a simple grey dress answered the door. "Is Mrs. Burnett expecting you?"

"Yes. I'm Stormi Nelson, and this is Maryann Steele. We have an appointment."

"This way, please. Mrs. Burnett is in the garden."

The very place I wanted to go. Excitement bubbled up in me. I didn't have time for gardening, but did enjoy the beauty of a well-tended lawn. Not to mention that the more work I had for Rusty, the less time he had to snoop in other people's windows.

Speaking of. I stopped short to see Rusty trimming a dead rose bush. Why was my gardener in Susan Burnett's garden?

"Miss Stormi?" Rusty brandished gardening shears in my direction. "Mrs. Burnett pay me ten dollars, too. I'm going to be rich."

"That's nice." I narrowed my eyes in Susan's direction.

She gave me a smug smile. "My gardener quit. I'm training Rusty to do things exactly the way I like them."

I did not like my friend working for a murder suspect. "Won't that be a conflict of interest?"

"How so?" She tilted her head.

"He worked for me first. If I want to build my garden to the type of standard necessary to compete against you—" She could fill in the blank.

"I didn't know you wanted a friendly competition. I thought you only wanted to join my club."

"What's wrong with both? Rusty, I'll pay you twelve dollars."

His eyes widened.

"Fifteen," Susan said.

"Twenty." I grinned. "You do realize that we aren't talking about twelve dollars, right? You have to add a zero to it. Rusty just doesn't understand money."

She seemed taken aback. "I can't afford that."

"So, you were taking advantage of him." I crossed my arms.

Her cheeks darkened under her carefully applied blush. "This is between me and Rusty."

"She's trying to cheat you, Rusty."

He tossed down the shears and stormed out. "Rusty is mad."

Susan huffed. "Now, I have to find someone else, and they'll charge a lot more. I don't think I want you in my club, Stormi."

"That's fine by me." I pulled the photographs of her from my purse. "Do these mean anything to you?"

She covered her mouth with a hand covered with a gardening glove. "How did you get these?"

I explained about Dixon and how I

know had all his files. "I doubt you hired him to take the photos."

She shoved them back at me. "These are over two years old. Nobody cares anymore."

"Isn't your ex-husband going to re-run for mayor?" Maryann asked. "That would make these important to someone."

I loved how my assistant's mind worked.

15

After our informative meeting with Susan, we headed back to my house so I could write another chapter, give my agent an update on the book, and go over the information Dakota found. My nephew hadn't arrived yet.

The one hour photo place must be running behind. I checked the pantry for supper, threw some ground turkey, cheese, salsa, and layered tortillas into a pan and stuck it in the oven. Supper was done.

While I wrote and answered emails, Maryann worked on stamping postcards on my latest release.

"Aunt Stormi!" Dakota barreled into my office. "There's a woman with a kid on the front porch."

I turned in my chair. "Excuse me?"

"It's me." Rachel stepped up behind him, holding the hand of the cutest little girl with Matt's eyes. "I'm headed off on a job. Since you seem bent on marrying her father, here's your trial period. Her name is Roxi. She no longer takes naps, only eats peanut butter and jelly and macaroni and cheese, and goes to bed at eight o'clock. With me. She won't sleep alone." She set a cotton candy colored suitcase on the floor, planted a quick kiss on the child's cheek, and left.

I stared at the girl with my mouth open. I started to say something, then clamped my mouth shut while Dakota and Maryann both looked as if Rachel had left an alien in our midst. Which, in a manner of speaking, she had.

"Call my mother," I told Maryann. Mom would know what to do. "Oh, and let Matt know his daughter is here. Dakota, put her suitcase in my room." While they scattered to do my bidding, I held my hand out to the child.

She came willingly and climbed into my lap. I was hopelessly in love from that moment. Still clueless, but in love.

"Here." Maryann thrust her Ipad at me. On the screen, colors swirled. "See?" She moved her finger, causing the colors to dance. "There's another app for numbers and letters. Matt, and your mother, are both on their way." She dashed back out as if I'd threatened to set her hair on fire.

"What do you like to talk about?" I gently tugged on a chestnut curl. "I don't have any toys in the house." I made a note to go shopping. I moved the child to a different chair, pushed it up to a small round table, and turned to see Matt standing in the doorway.

Tears ran down his cheeks. He didn't speak, just stared at his daughter. His throat worked for a few seconds before words emerged. "She's beautiful."

"Just like her daddy," I said. "Roxi, this is your daddy."

She looked up and smiled. That was all it took.

Matt rushed to her side and swept her in his arms.

My throat clogged with tears, and I

glanced up to meet Mom's gaze.

"I've always wanted another grandchild," she said, her eyes shimmering.

We were all a bunch of saps.

Matt glanced at me. "I can't stay."

"I know. She'll be fine."

He pulled me close, sandwiching Roxi between us, and kissed me. It felt right, somehow, that there was a child.

"I'll be back by supper."

I nodded and stepped back as Mom took Roxi from his arms. "We'll go buy some toys."

"Oh, let me." Mom snuggled her close. "What fun!"

Just like that, they all left. Funny how lonely I felt. Roxi had been here less than half an hour and already the room felt empty. Maybe I was meant to be a mother after all.

"Wow." Maryann came back into my office.

"Wow is right." I plopped into my chair. Writing was the least thing on my mind. "Does Dakota have his pictures?"

"Right here." He squeezed past

Maryann and spread them out on the table. "I didn't want to bring them in while the kid was here. She might have gotten them dirty."

I bit back a grin. "You also said you found out some other information."

"Yep." He glanced up. "There's a small online magazine that follows the local elections pretty closely. Mayor Burnett is in the middle of a smear campaign with that plastic surgeon. You wouldn't believe all the stuff they're saying about each other. My guess…the former mayor plastered the doc's face on that picture. Now, she's out to get him good."

He tapped the photos he'd taken today. "Cheryl Miller seems to have forgotten all about the principal and moved on. This is quite the seedy town, Aunt Stormi."

"I'm beginning to agree with you." Especially after all that had happened over the last year. "While your information is amazing, we're still no closer to finding Dixon's killer." We had enough suspects to form a baseball team.

He nodded. "I'll keep digging, but I'm placing bets on Burnett or Pritchard. They have the most to lose."

"I agree." Now, to figure out our next move.

"Let's go over our suspects. Cheryl Miller is upset that Principal Miller won't leave his wife. Not really a strong motive to kill Dixon when compared to the others. Hank Caldwell is scum, but again, not a strong motive. Susan Burnett's ex-husband wants to rerun for mayor. Pritchard and the ex-mayor are running against each other. It's a hodge-podge."

Maryann perched on the corner of the desk. "Some of the people on this list aren't actually the ones who hired Dixon. So...how did they find out it was Dixon surveilling them?"

"Someone snitched," Dakota said.

"But who and why?" I paced the room. "Since Pritchard has hired me, let's focus on her and Burnett for now." I speared my nephew with a stern look. "I don't want you ditching school, but go ahead and continue snooping." People tended to overlook kids. He might get closer than either I or the police could.

My laptop dinged, alerting me to an email. I opened it. "Got an email from Caldwell. He wants fifty thousand dollars to do the attic. That sounds reasonable." I'd still run it past Matt, but with Caldwell under my roof, I'd be able to watch him. "What would be his motive for killing Dixon?"

The other two thought for a minute, then Maryann spoke up. "Maybe he's afraid it will hurt his business? Oak Meadows is a small town. People talk."

I grinned. "Yes, they do. I need to talk to Rusty and Mrs. Rogers." Those two knew more about the people of this town than anyone. "You two hold down the fort."

Since Rusty seemed to be off sulking somewhere after Susan's attempts to cheat him out of his money, I jogged across the street and knocked on Mrs. Rogers's door.

"What?" She yanked open the door.

We might have faced down a killer together, but the woman still didn't like me. "You answered the door mighty fast. Were you spying on me?"

"Who's the child?"

"My soon-to-be stepdaughter. My turn. What do you know about the people on this list?"

She glanced at the paper in my hand. "Come on in. I'll make tea."

This had to be a first. I followed her into a surprisingly modern house. I expected floral print furniture and doilies. Instead, her house looked as if all came from IKEA.

"Sit at the table." She pointed to a small dinette set and bustled around the kitchen making tea. Once she had a stainless steel pot on the stove, she sat across from me. "Did one of these people kill Dixon?"

"Possibly. Did you know him?"

"Yep. Didn't like him either. He is, or was, my former son-in-law."

That was a bombshell I didn't expect. "Tell me about him."

"He was always out to make a quick buck, no matter who might get hurt in the process. He got so many death threats, my Becky got scared and filed for divorce. She's remarried with two kids." She narrowed her eyes. "I didn't know Detective Steele had a child."

"Neither did we. Don't get off topic."

She shrugged. "Fine. Caldwell is a philanderer, Pritchard is a whore, Miller is a two-timer, don't get me started on his mistress, and Burnett is a whiny scared of her shadow slip of a woman."

"Please do get started on Cheryl Miller."

"Crazy as a bat." She got up and removed the whistling pot from the stove, talking as she poured hot water over tea bags. "Told everyone in town that her and that principal were married. Nobody believed her, or course. I sure am glad I don't have any kids in his school. I don't know how the real Mrs. Miller puts up with him." She waved a spoon at me. "He might have killed Dixon to save his marriage. Who knows? Of course, Cheryl might have killed Dixon to protect her fantasy."

She set a steaming cup of tea in front of me. "They all have the same motive. To keep Dixon's material from getting out." She smiled a sinister smile. "But, it is out, isn't it? I bet you have it."

"I do." I smiled over the rim of my cup.

"I don't know why you put yourself in danger when you could be writing those smut books of yours."

"I don't write smut, and you know it." I motioned my head to her coffee table. "Would you like me to sign the book?"

"I only bought it because I'm in it. But, yes, please sign it before you leave."

I think the two of us had taken a giant step forward in our relationship. "Do me a favor, okay? Keep your eyes and ears open? Let me know if you find out anything that might alert me to Dixon's killer." I sipped the tea, a pleasing blend of orange and cranberry.

"I never figured your man to commit fornication, other than cavorting with you on the front porch, anyway."

So, we were back to Roxi. "It was a long time ago. I trust him."

"That's what they all say. Men can't be trusted." She glanced at the window where Rusty peered in. "I thought you were going to stop that behavior."

"I tried." I opened the window. "What?"

"Big man at your house. He yelled at the yellow-haired girl."

"Caldwell yelled at Maryann? What did he say?"

"To tell you to stay out of his business and he wasn't going to fix your house." Rusty turned and trotted away.

I sighed. Now, I'd have to find a new contractor.

"My son can do renovations." Mrs. Rogers opened a small porcelain box next to her phone and pulled out a business card. She handed it to me. "Tell him we know each other and he'll give you a good deal."

"Thank you." I glanced at the card. Roger's Construction. Through the front window, I noticed Matt's car pull up. I frowned. He shouldn't be home yet. "Thank you for the information and the tea." I took another sip and let myself out.

I hurried across the street and met Matt as he was getting out of his truck. "What's wrong?" The palor of his face told me he didn't have good news. "Mom?

Angela?"

"No." He pulled me into his arms. "Rachel was in a car accident. She didn't make it."

"She's dead?" I peered up into his face.

"Yes. Roxi is now officially ours." He let go of me and ran his hands through his hair. "Rachel ran into a tree when her tire blew out. The medical examiner says she died on impact, so that's something."

"I'm sorry." I cupped his cheek.

"I'm sorry for Roxi. She's so young, she won't remember her mother, and I don't know enough about Rachel anymore to keep the memory alive."

"I'll find as many back issues of magazines with her photos in them as I can. We'll keep them for Roxi."

"You'd do that?"

"I'll do anything for you." I wrapped my arms around his neck and gave Mrs. Rogers something else to talk about.

16

I moved my office to a corner of my bedroom, at least until the attic renovations were complete, and turned the former office into a pink and purple room fit for a princess. Matt kept his daughter most nights at his house, but with his work schedule, I'd been her primary caregiver for the last three days.

After asking a few times where Mommy was, Roxi had settled into a sort of routine. I wished I could say the same. Instead, I sat across the kitchen table from her and watched her eat oatmeal sweetened with raw sugar.

Mom had gotten rid of the child's refusal to eat but a couple of items right off by using bribery. She kept a cupcake in plain sight. Eat your dinner and the cupcake was yours. Roxi, being the smart little thing she was, caught on quick.

"I really need to work today," I said, sipping my regular creamed to a pale brown, coffee.

"Play," Roxi responded with a dimpled grin.

"No, work. So, the problem is…what do I do with you?" Everyone else was gone, either to school or work. Not only did I need to do some writing, but I needed to do some investigating. "There's no help for it. You're going to have to come along. You and Aunt Maryann can stay in the car while I do the grunt work." I could leave them both at home, but I needed my assistant to take notes.

"That should be all right." Maryann grabbed a rag and cleaned Roxi's face and hands. "She won't be out of either one of our sights."

Good. I trusted Maryann's instincts where children were concerned. She'd been a teacher for almost ten years. "We'll pay Susan Burnett a visit first, then try and speak with her ex-husband. If we still have time, we'll try for a meeting with Pritchard." I stood and set my mug in the sink.

"Great. I'll pack Roxi a lunch and be ready in fifteen minutes."

"I'm glad you're here. I wouldn't have thought to pack her a lunch. I'm going to make a horrible mother."

"You'll settle in and be just fine." Maryann set her niece on the floor. "I need to get off work early tonight. Michael and I have a date."

"Your hours are your own." Matt was working, Mom was going out with her boyfriend, Angela with Wayne…that left me alone, again, with Roxi. I guess I was getting a crash course on motherhood.

Twenty minutes later, the trunk of my car packed full of child things, and Roxi strapped into her car seat, we headed back toward Susan Burnett's mansion on the hill. If she wasn't the one blackmailing Pritchard, then she knew who was. I still didn't know if the blackmail had anything to do with Dixon's death, but it was worth digging into.

I pulled the car as close to the front

door as possible and rolled down the car windows. Maryann stepped out with me and positioned herself next to the rear door. Susan would have to step outside to talk with us this time. I banged the knocker and waited.

The same woman in grey answered the door. "Please, come in."

"No, I need Mrs. Burnett to step out here this time, thank you."

The maid frowned. "Very well. Please wait."

I was starting to think Susan wasn't going to grace us with her presence by the time she joined us. When she did, the look on her face said she'd prefer to be anywhere but there.

"What?" She glared and crossed her arms. "I thought we spoke about all we needed to."

I slapped the photo of Pritchard down on the trunk of the car. "I need you to look at this."

She sighed dramatically and glanced at the photo. Her eyes widened. "I don't know anything about what that woman does."

"This picture has been Photoshopped. This woman isn't Amanda Pritchard. Since Lincoln is running against her for mayor, it leads me to believe that the two of you have the most to gain by tarnishing her reputation."

Susan gave an unladylike snort. "As if her reputation can be tarnished further. I still didn't have anything to do with altering that photo."

"You wouldn't want her out of the running so you could get back with Lincoln and be Oak Meadows' first lady again?"

"My personal life is none of your business." Spots of color appeared under her makeup.

"Mama!" Roxi hung out the window, having somehow escaped her carseat. "Potty."

Susan froze. "You have a child?"

"She's Matt's. Long story." I pulled Roxi through the window. "May we use your restroom?"

"I've always wanted a child."

The way she looked at Roxi made me uneasy. I clutched the little one tighter until she protested. "Susan?"

She seemed to shake herself free of her musings. "Of course. I'll show you where it is."

I motioned to Maryann to follow, and mouthed for her to keep an eye on our reluctant hostess.

Susan led us down a marble-tiled hall to a bathroom as big as Roxi's new bedroom. Everything in the room was white and polished nickel. "Take all the time you need," she said, closing the double doors.

"I'll wait right here." Maryann crossed her arms and spread her legs like a hired guard.

I sat Roxi on the toilet and started snooping. Usually the little girl took her time, swinging her legs and singing, but since we were in someone's place that I wanted to take a closer look at, I was afraid fate would intervene and she'd conclude her business faster than usual.

I made a beeline for the medicine cabinet. Bingo! A full bottle of anti-depressants. I checked the prescription date. Almost a month ago. Through research, I knew what happened to people who didn't take their meds. They went bonkers.

"She's coming back." Maryann knocked on the door.

I replaced the pill bottle and turned to Roxi. "Finished, sweetie?"

"Yep." She hopped down and pulled up the ruffled tights I'd purchased for her. "I'm hungry."

"We'll eat in the car." I took her hand and stepped back into the hall where Susan waited with Maryann. "Thank you."

She eyed Roxi as if the child were a slice of cake. "Of course. Children are our most precious resource."

Right. "Let us know if you find out who might be blackmailing Pritchard." I walked away as fast as Roxi's legs would move.

Back in the car, with Roxi buckled in tighter, I turned to Maryann. "Am I the only one creeped out by the way she looked at Roxi?"

"No, it was strange." She unwrapped a package of peanut-butter crackers and handed them over the seat to her niece.

"But, I've seen that look on faces of women unable to have children before."

"I'm probably overreacting, as usual." I took one last glance to where Susan stared from the doorway of her house, then drove down the curving drive toward town and Burnett's business offices.

The man owned several Savings and Loans, one of which was in our fair town, and housed his home office. I parked in front of the red-brick building and unbuckled Roxi. Having a child took twice as long to get anything done.

The three of us trooped into the modern reception area. Maryann and Roxi took seats in the waiting area while I flashed my PI badge and asked to see Mr. Burnett.

The receptionist, who looked as if she indulged in Pritchard's services one too many times, pursed her collagen enhanced lips. "I'll see if he's available. Please, have a seat."

I filled a paper cone with water from a nearby cooler, took a drink, then refilled and handed it to Roxi. Maybe I could do this mother thing after all. I second-guessed when she upended the cone over her clothes.

A blast of cool air met us as someone pushed open the double glass doors. Cheryl Miller, looking a little more put together than the last time I'd seen her, even as far as wearing expensive-looking jewelry, stormed in and approached the receptionist. "Someone has made a mistake with my account."

"I'll get you an account manager, Miss Miller. Please have a seat."

Cheryl huffed and turned. Spotting us, she rushed toward us and scooped Roxi into her arms. "Whose little darling is this?"

"Matt's." I took Roxi back. "You shouldn't pick up other people's children."

She gave a wry smile. "I heard of how an ex of his kept the child a secret." She put a finger to her lips. "I wonder...hmmm. That might just work for me." She chucked Roxi under the chin and sashayed to a nearby chair.

"Does every parent have to worry about someone snatching their child the way it seems?" I stared across the room at Cheryl, but spoke to Maryann.

"I hope not. This has been a very strange day."

"Miss Nelson, Mr. Burnett will see you now," the receptionist said.

"Keep one hand on Roxi at all times," I told Maryann. "I'll make this quick."

The receptionist directed me three doors down. I knocked on one with a brass placard that read, "Lincoln Burnett", then entered when invited.

The man was extremely attractive for his age. Dark hair, peppered with grey. Blue eyes that could see right through a person. Cleft in his chin. He must have been a heart breaker when he was young. He pasted on a grin and held out a hand for me to shake. "What can I do for you, Miss Nelson? You're a local celebrity in this town."

"Thank you, but I'm afraid I'm here today as a private investigator." I sat in a chair opposite his leather one and pulled the altered photo from my purse. I slid it across his desk. "I'm wondering whether you know anything about this."

He sat in his chair and perched a pair of reading glasses on his nose. "That's priceless. May I have it?"

"No." I snatched it back. "The photo isn't real, Mr. Burnett."

His smile faded. "Are you saying I would resort to blackmail to win this election?"

"Would you?" I raised my eyebrows.

"I cannot believe you would have the gall to come into my place of business and accuse me of such a low act." He planted palms flat on the desk and stood. "I'm going to have to ask you to leave."

"You have yet to deny my allegations." I refused to shrink back under the hard glint in his eyes.

"Miss Nelson." His tone grew colder by several degrees. "I'm denying your allegations. Ms. Pritchard is a..." He sighed. "I won't besmirch her to you. Ask anyone else and you'll receive the same answer I would give. I'll win this election without resorting to underhanded means. If you were to ask around about me, you'll find that I am an upstanding citizen of this town. Other than my divorce, there isn't a black mark to be found."

"If not you, then who would benefit?"

"My crazy ex-wife? One of Pritchard's many liasons? Take your pick."

I really felt as if I could cross his name off my suspect list. I wasn't always hitting homeruns, but my gut told me that despite the man's cold demeanor at being questioned, he was telling the truth.

I thrust out my hand. "My apologies. Thank you for talking with me."

He returned the handshake. "Miss Nelson, be careful. Whoever killed Dixon wants something kept hidden. If you go around asking questions, you're only putting yourself in danger."

Just like that, he was back on my suspect list. "I'll be careful." I stepped out of his office and ran smack dab into Mom's boyfriend, Jerry.

"Good afternoon, Stormi." He leaned on a wheeled dolly piled with boxes. "Fancy running into you."

"Do you come here often?"

"Every day."

I got a brilliant idea.

17

The authorities released Dixon's body and I woke the next morning preparing for a funeral. I hoped to gather information, since murderers often attended the service of those they killed.

"You did what?" Matt frowned. "I know I didn't hear you correctly when you said you went snooping with my daughter in tow?"

"Since I seem to be her primary caregiver, how else am I going to work? We kept her in the car—"

"We?" His face darkened.

"Maryann and I. Between the two of us, she was perfectly safe. Although, Susan Burnett and Cheryl Miller did seem very curious in her." I handed him a mug of fresh coffee.

"Two murder suspects have taken an interest in my daughter?" He set the mug down without taking a sip. "Maybe we should postpone our wedding until you settle more into the role of a mother."

My heart plummeted. "Are you serious? Wouldn't a better solution be to find a babysitter?" I didn't want to think he was serious, but the look on his face said he was very serious.

"She just lost her mother, Stormi. She doesn't need to be foisted off on daycare." He shook his head. "No, Maryann is going to have to stop working for you for a while and take care of my daughter."

Tears stung my eyes. I knew Rachel's death, and Matt acquiring a daughter would change my life, but I didn't anticipate it spiraling downward. "Are you serious? I'll not investigate anymore until Mom is home to watch Roxi. I need Maryann with me."

He turned a tortured look my way. "We'll talk about this again after the funeral." He glanced at his watch and stormed out the front door.

Feeling very much like a scolded puppy, I followed and climbed into the front passenger seat. We didn't need to worry about Roxi, since Mom elected to stay behind and babysit. Maybe, I could start dropping Roxi off at the bakery when I needed to leave the house.

We didn't speak on the way to the funeral home and pulled into the parking lot at the same time as Maryann and Michael. Maryann took one look at me and Matt and shook her head, mouthing that she'd talk to me later.

I nodded, slipped my arm through Matt's stiff one, and allowed him to lead me into the building and take a seat in the back. Somehow, I needed to make things right so our wedding could get back on track.

Dixon's casket took up prominence at the front of the room. A red-eyed, tear-stained faced Jordyn, the barista, sobbed over the casket. No one else approached the body, but all the suspects were there, sitting in pews and staring straight ahead. Them, and us, were the only so-called mourners. How sad.

A few seconds later, Dixon's daughter slipped through a side door and sat in a corner. April's face was pale, but no tears ran down her cheeks. How sad. She'd never had the chance to make amends with her father. I could relate in her loss only as far as to say my father had been murdered. Other than that, we had nothing in common. I'd loved my father with every fiber of my being.

A man in a dark gray suit approached the podium, said a few generic words about death, closed with a prayer and asked if anyone wanted to say a few words. The room quieted as if holding its breath. No one got out of their seat. No one looked at each other. When it became uncomfortably obvious that no one had anything to say, we were dismissed.

I had hoped someone would get up, if only to bad mouth Dixon. Instead, I left the building feeling sad that no one seemed to care a man was dead.

Matt slipped his hand into mine. "I'm sorry. I know you're doing the best you can." He turned me to face him. "I worry so much about you out there snooping, then to find out you took Roxi—"

"I promise she was safe the entire time. But, it won't happen again. I'll leave her at the bakery if I have to. Mom will give her some dough to play with."

"Thank you." He flashed the smile that never failed to melt my heart. "I don't want to push back our wedding. You know I'd marry you this instance if you were to say the word."

Just like that, all was right with my world once again. I snuggled close to him. "Come to supper tonight and meet Mom's boyfriend."

"I will. This investigation is going nowhere. A night off will do me good. Maybe I'll think of something."

He drove me home and headed off to squeeze in a few hours of work. I watched him go then headed across the street to see why Mrs. Rogers was frantically waving.

"Do you have something?" I asked.

She pulled me into her house. "That new barista was dating Dixon. No one seems to know anything about her, but I found out something, thanks to that gardener of yours. She seems to spend some time with Lincoln Burnett, too."

"Do tell." Excitement welled.

"Yep." She shook her head hard enough to wobble the curlers in her hair. "Before that, she dated Caldwell. I think that gal might know something. She hasn't shown up at Delicious Aroma for three days. Folks say she's hiding."

"She was at the funeral."

"Drat. I wanted to go to that. Anything exciting happen?"

"Nothing. People just sat there, then left. No one other than Jordyn even went up to the coffin."

"Not a successful funeral. Too bad."

"Rusty gave you the information on Jordyn?"

"I had to pay him ten dollars to get him to talk. That boy is tight-lipped."

While approaching the age of forty, folks still looked at Rusty as a boy. Maybe it was his childlike attitude. I worried about him poking his nose in other people's business, but he did dig up information others overlooked. "Where is Rusty now?"

"Poking around in your tool shed, last

I saw."

I glanced across the street. "Thanks. I'll catch you later." I jogged back across the street and to my backyard.

As I approached the tool shed, I ducked a shovel and gardening shears. "Rusty?"

"Yep."

"Would you mind telling me why you're chucking my things into the yard?"

"Looking for camera."

"I don't have a camera in there."

"Rusty does."

All right, I wouldn't ask.

"Found." He came out, covered in dust, and clutching a rather new looking digital camera. "Dakota gave me a present."

"Did he tell you to hide it?"

He nodded. "This is the best place. Very messy."

Cleaning my tool shed was not a priority. "What kind of pictures are on there?"

He thrust the camera at me.

I turned it on and scanned the photos. One after another were of Jordyn. One showed her snooping in Dixon's house, despite the crime scene tape. Been there, done that. Another showed her having drinks at the same biker bar where I'd made new friends. The last photo showed her in what seemed a heated conversation with Lincoln Burnett. Clearly, the woman was looking for something.

"What made you watch Jordyn?"

"Dakota."

Ah. Since my nephew had to go to school, he had Rusty doing his snooping. "You did good. These are great. May I borrow the camera?"

He seemed uncertain. "What if you lose it?"

"I won't. I'll print off the photos, then give the camera back. Will that work?"

"Yep."

"Clean this up, okay?" I patted him on the shoulder and hurried into the house.

Mom and Roxi sat at the kitchen table playing with giant sized Legos. I gave them both a kiss and made a beeline for my office. I knew Rusty enough to know that if I didn't return the camera soon, he'd start whining about me stealing the thing. Five minutes later, I had two prints of each photo and the camera back in Rusty's hands.

"Mom, I need to drop Roxi off at the bakery tomorrow while I interview someone, okay?" Back in the kitchen, I opened the fridge and pulled out a soda.

"I guess that will be all right. Mercy!" She glanced at the clock. "Help Roxi put these away. I need to check the ham and get into the shower. Jerry will be here in an hour."

"I hope you don't mind, but I'm going to ask for his help with Lincoln Burnett."

That stopped her in her tracks. "I said I didn't want him to know the dangers I sometimes get in."

"He makes deliveries there every day. It will be harmless enough."

Her eyes narrowed. "I like this man, Stormi. Don't get him killed." She rushed down the stairs to the basement, forgetting all about the ham.

I set a box at Roxi's feet. "Put the Legos in here while I check on supper, okay, sweetie? See how much noise you can make."

She grinned and threw one after the other into the box with loud clanks.

The ham seemed to be fine. I quickly peeled potatoes and put them on to boil, then opened a few cans of corn. Biscuits would be nice. While I worked on getting our meal prepared, Roxi scooted the box of Legos around the kitchen and made car noises. See? I could totally do this domestic/mother thing.

Five o'clock on the dot and friends and family trooped through the front door. Matt headed straight for the kitchen, kissed his daughter, then wrapped his arms around me. "Smells good."

"Supper is almost ready."

He nuzzled my neck. "I meant you. You smell like biscuits."

I giggled and pulled away. "Behave and help Roxi put that box in her room."

"Mama has spoken." He scooped his daughter in one arm and the box in the other and left me feeling shocked, loved, and warm.

Mama. I liked the sound of that very much.

"Hello, again." Jerry entered the room. "Where's my girl?"

"Making herself beautiful." I tilted my head. "I'd like to ask you do to do something. Remember the first night you were here when you said you might have to get involved in one of our adventures?"

He nodded, reaching for a biscuit. "Sure do."

"I really hope you're tight-lipped, Jerry. This is important."

"I can keep a secret."

I took a deep breath. "Lincoln Burnett is a suspect in a murder investigation."

His eyes widened, but instead of saying anything, he popped the biscuit into his mouth.

"Since you're there every day making deliveries, I'd like you to do a bit of snooping. See if you can find out anything Lincoln might have had against Dixon or Doctor Amanda Pritchard."

"You don't have to do this," Mom said, closing the basement door. "It might be dangerous."

"Sounds exciting." He kissed her. "Of course, I'll help. I might be a delivery man now, but I served twenty years in the army. Life has gotten a bit routine. You girls are just what this old man needs."

I turned away from their affection. I wanted Mom happy, really I did, but it was hard to see her with anyone but Dad. "If you're found out, you will be in danger, if Lincoln is the killer. I don't think he is, but he definitely is playing dirty in the mayor election."

"So, you're basically hoping I can ferret out what he has against Pritchard and anything else is a bonus?"

"Exactly." I turned with a grin.

"Shouldn't be too hard. No one accompanies me when I put deliveries straight into the supply closet. I doubt they'll look twice if I do a bit of wandering. I can make myself invisible when I need to."

I doubted it, considering his looks and size, but I was willing to take all the help I could get.

18

The next morning I dropped Roxi off at the bakery and headed to the coffee shop to talk to Jordyn. Tyler told us she'd quit. The next stop was the address she'd used in her file. If Oak Meadows had a slum, the house was smack dab in the middle.

A silver Toyota Corolla sat in the driveway. I had no idea whether she actually lived there. I shoved open my door, squared my shoulders, and marched to the front door.

I lifted my hand to knock, and got only air.

"Get in here before you get us all killed." Jordyn didn't look anything like a barista at that moment. Her dark hair was pulled back into a severe ponytail. She wore dark jeans with a black tee shirt. A gun nested in a holster on her hip.

"Who are you?" I eyed the gun.

"Jordyn Townsend, undercover from Little Rock PD." She crossed her arms. "You are seriously impeding my investigation."

"Into whom?" I wouldn't let her attitude deter me. While her identity cast a mountain size nugget of surprise on my head, I was still hired by Dakota and Pritchard to find answers.

"Dixon. Have a seat." She fell into a patched leather chair and motioned for us to sit on a torn, stained sofa. "Pardon the mess, but I'm renting and it came furnished."

"No worries here." Maryann and I gave identical looks at a suspicious rust colored stain next to what looked like a bullet hole. "I'm not here to judge."

"You cried at Dixon's funeral," Maryann said.

"I'm a good actress." Jordyn gave a wry smile. "Have to keep up pretenses."

"Why were you surveilling Dixon?" I perched on the edge of the sofa on a spot that looked clean compared to the rest.

"People weren't necessarily hiring him to spy on their significant others."

"He was blackmailing them." It started to make sense. "That's why he was killed. Who do you think is the perp?"

"I haven't narrowed it down." She smiled again. "I'm sure you know everything I do."

I wanted to discuss her with Matt before giving away too much information. I'd run across my share of bad cops and had my heart broken because of it. My second case involved Matt's partner who covered for his gangster cousin and sacrificed his life for me in the end. Wayne, Matt's new partner had proven himself trustworthy time and time again, but I didn't know this hard woman in front of me.

As if she could read my mind, she said, "You don't trust me. That's all right. You might stay alive longer that way."

"If Dixon was blackmailing people, why does that put me in danger? I'm only trying to clear someone's reputation of a black mark."

"Poking your nose where it doesn't belong, you mean."

As if I hadn't heard that before. "Dixon did a good job convincing people he was hired to snoop."

"Not that good. He's dead." Jordyn stood. "I'm willing to work with you on this, Stormi, but you have to trust me. I know you're going to talk to Detective Steele before making a decision. Here's my number." She handed me a card. "Call at any time. Oh, and tell that old lady who lives across the street from you to stop following me around. I'd hate for something to happen to her."

"You know where I live?"

"I know a lot about you. You're quite the talk of the LRPD." She laughed. "Some good, some bad, but we all know who you are."

I wasn't sure whether I should be pleased or outraged. I chose apathy and slid her card into my pocket. "Thank you for your time." I stood and led Maryann out of the house.

"I never would have guessed she was a cop," Maryann said, sliding into the car.

"She looks kind of young."

"Which made her the perfect undercover cop." I drove us home, intending to talk to Jerry and Mrs. Rogers. One to get information, the other to warn about snooping. My old neighbor might be crusty, but I'd hate for anything to happen to her.

I pulled into the driveway and waved at the Olsens. He grinned back while his wife glowered. She never could quite get over the fact that the entire female population of our town wasn't after her balding, overweight husband. She shooed him into the house with a broom like he was an escaped chicken. My neighbors were a constant source of entertainment.

"The Salazars are back," Maryann pointed out.

"Hey, Tony, Becky," I said, climbing from the car. "How was your trip?"

Tony rushed toward me on his bowed legs. Being little people, I never knew whether they actually went on vacation or to the hospital for yet another surgery on their poor skeleton. "Wonderful. What's been happening around here? Anyone keeping up the Neighborhood Watch?"

"No one other than me, and there's a lot to tell you."

"I'll take Watch tonight and have you fill me in before I go. It's good to be back." He grinned and toddled back to haul a suitcase into the house.

When I'd moved into my neighborhood of renovated Victorian homes and ranchers, I'd thought it the perfect location. Had I known how death thrived in even such a seemingly peaceful subdivision, I might have thought twice. To think it had all started because my agent told me to get out more. That reclusive writer was no more. Now, I went looking for my stories and dodged bullets in the process. Oh, how times have changed. How I've changed.

Mom, Jerry, and Roxi sat in the kitchen having cookies and milk. I paused in the doorway to watch Mom dote on not only her boyfriend, but her new grandchild. Matt and I might not have tied the knot yet, but it was easy to see his daughter already had a large piece of Mom's heart.

"Just the woman I want to see," Jerry boomed. "Sit a spell."

"I think I will." I pulled up a chair while Maryann did the same. "Did you find out something?"

"Well, Lincoln Burnett is closed up tighter than a clam, but his receptionist isn't immune to my charms." He grinned and winked at Mom.

"Who is, dear?" Mom planted a quick kiss on his cheek.

I squelched my impatience and waited for the love birds to stop the gushy stuff. In the meantime, I broke another cookie in half for Roxi.

"Okay, enough stalling." Jerry leaned his elbows on the table. "It seems Lincoln has had a lot of women visitors this week. Among them were…Cheryl Miller, Amanda Pritchard, and Jordyn…somebody. Miller caused quite the ruckus because a few thousand dollars disappeared from her account, most likely taken by Lance Miller. Since his name was also on the account, the Savings and Loan won't do anything about it. Things got quite heated and she told Burnett that he would be sorry.

"Amanda Pritchard accused him of trying to sabotage her campaign and playing dirty. She also threatened him." He shook his head. "There are a lot of angry women in this town. Now, the barista...she's a different story. She went into his office, came out grinning, and he followed a few minutes later looking as if he'd lost his dog. My words, not the receptionist. I saw that particular episode. Then, Lincoln burnt rubber out of the parking lot. Rather suspicious, don't you think?"

"Very." The only suspect absent from the drama was Caldwell. Maybe the man was nothing more than the jerk he appeared to be. I put him at the bottom of my suspect list. "This was a big help, Jerry. Thank you."

"Anytime, young lady. Playing spy is fun. I hadn't enjoyed a day at work as much in a long time."

"Did you learn anything new today, Stormi?" Mom handed me a glass of milk and two cookies.

"The new barista is actually a cop

investigating Dixon who, it turns out, was not hired to snoop, but was, in actuality, blackmailing everyone on his list." I dipped my chocolate chip cookie into my milk.

"I still say you should have been a cop." Matt strolled into the room and nuzzled my neck. "Sorry I didn't tell you about Townsend, but I couldn't." He moved on to lift Roxi and toss her into the air.

She squealed with delight and grabbed fistfuls of hair with hands covered in cookie crumbs and melted chocolate chips. "Daddy."

"How I love to hear that word."

Probably as much as I loved seeing him happy. "I understand about Jordyn. You can't tell me everything. She wants my help."

He set Roxi back in her seat. "Absolutely not. She's known for getting into trouble. Kind of like you, in that regard. The two of you are a mixture of combustible materials. Then, add Maryann into the mix and boom!"

"Hey." She glanced up from her own

cookies and milk. "I just follow along, take notes, and give fresh perspective."

"Sure you do."

"Are you home for a while?" I asked, finishing off the treat. "I need to run across the street and talk to Mrs. Rogers."

"Go ahead. I'm here for supper, then Roxi and I will head home. It's bath night."

He sounded so much like a father it warmed me to the bone. I couldn't wait to have children with him. Babies he could experience from day one. I kissed him. "Be right back."

Mrs. Rogers had the front door open before I could knock. "It's about time. I've been on pins and needles all day waiting for you to show up."

"I came to ask you to stop snooping on orders of Little Rock PD."

She snorted. "As if I'd listen to big city cops. They're all as crooked as your morals. I guess you've been talking to that barista."

"As a matter of fact, yes. She's a cop."

"Not a very good one. She never did

ditch me." Mrs. Rogers cackled. "Anyway, she isn't the one I wanted you here to talk about. That Cheryl Miller is going around town saying that she's out to kill someone."

"Yes, Lance, for cleaning out her bank account."

"Is that all?" She slumped onto a chair. "I thought for sure she knocked off Dixon." She exhaled heavily. "So, who's the killer?"

"I don't know yet, but—" a sound outside the sliding glass doors alerted me to danger.

A figure in black aimed a gun at Mrs. Rogers.

I tackled my neighbor to the ground as the gun went off. As I stared in horror through the shattered glass, Rusty tackled the assailant. They struggled. The gun went off again, and Rusty lay still as the figure in black dashed out of sight.

"Rusty!" I scrambled on hands and knees, unmindful of the glass, to his side and rolled him over.

Blood spread across his midsection. "I'm shot."

"I know. Mrs. Rogers is calling the ambulance." I ripped off my shirt, shivering in the spaghetti strap undershirt I wore. I pressed the tee shirt against his side and prayed the bullet hadn't punctured his stomach. "Don't you die on me, Rusty."

"I'll try not to."

"The ambulance is on its way." Mrs. Rogers knelt next to us and slid a throw pillow under Rusty's head. "Son, you probably saved our lives. I've been watching you for a while now, and once the doctors patch you up good, I think you need to come and live with me. You need someone to keep you from doing foolish things."

He nodded and closed his eyes.

"Look at me, Rusty." I glanced up as Matt, gun drawn, sprinted around the corner of the house.

"Let me see." He shoved my hands away and ripped open Rusty's flannel shirt. "Thank you, God. It's a flesh wound. Rusty will live to peek in another window." He grabbed me to his side. "When I heard the gun go off…"

"I know." I wrapped my arms around his middle and held on.

"Girl, I'm never going to try and run you out of town again," Mrs. Rogers said. "Detective, she tackled me down like an all-star. If not, she'd be wearing my brains right now."

Eew.

19

After surgery to remove his spleen and sew him up from the bullet, Rusty drifted in and out of consciousness. During a moment that was lucid for Rusty, I gripped his hand. "You have to stop jumping in front of bullets. One of these times, you won't be lucky." First Mom, during one of the scariest times in our life when Cherokee had been kidnapped by a sex trafficking ring, and now for Mrs. Rogers.

"It's what Jesus would do," he mumbled.

"You're right." I caressed his hand. "You'll like living with Mrs. Rogers. She'll treat you like a king."

"That's right, boy." Mrs. Rogers

bustled into the room. "Stormi, go find the shooter. I'll take care of this young man."

"Shooter is a woman," Rusty said.

"How do you know?" I paused halfway from standing.

"I felt...girl parts." His face reddened.

Just like that, my suspect list was down to two. "Good job." I patted his shoulder. "I'll stop back later with six of Mom's cupcakes."

I left the hospital and headed for the police station. The moment I entered the front door, Angela leaped from behind the reception desk and dragged me into a corner. "What?" I yanked free.

"Things are happening around here. Matt and Wayne storm around like it's the end of the world. That undercover cop, the barista? Well, she came in here yesterday yelling loud enough that I could hear her through the conference room door. Now, she's missing." She whispered the last word.

"She's in hiding."

"I'm not so sure. Rumors are she might be dead." Again with the harsh whisper.

"Where was she seen last?"

"That biker bar on Highway 64." She glanced over her shoulder as the conference room door opened. "I've got to get back to work. Be careful."

I nodded and met Matt halfway down the hall. "Got a minute?"

"That's about all I've got."

"Rusty said the shooter was female. He felt her girl parts when he tackled her."

Despite the situation, a smile tugged at Matt's lips. "Poor guy."

"It isn't funny. It's the best lead we've had in a long time."

"It is that." He steered me outside to my car. "I want you to take extra care. Don't go anywhere without your gun. Things are heating up, and Roxi doesn't need to lose another mother."

"Is Roxi the only one who will miss me?"

He pulled me in for a kiss. "Not at all."

"I'll be careful. You do the same."

"As much as I hate to say this, go get Maryann. I don't want you going anywhere alone. Not even the hospital."

I nodded. "I'm heading to the biker bar on 64." I held up a hand to halt his protests. "The leader is a huge fan of mine. I'm in absolutely no danger there. I'll call you when I'm done."

"Wayne and I just came from there."

"Those men won't talk to the cops and you know it."

He gave me another kiss. "Be careful."

"I will." I climbed into the driver's seat and blew him a kiss. I turned the key in the ignition. Nothing but a click. I started to turn the key again, but the hairs on my arms stood up. I rolled down my window. "Matt? My car won't start."

The tone of my voice must have alerted him to the possible seriousness of the situation. "Don't move." He yanked his radio from his belt. "Possible car bomb in the parking lot. Make it fast."

A bomb? My insides turned to liquid. "What do I do?"

"Nothing." He carefully lifted the door handle and opened the door. "Do. Not. Move." He knelt next to the car and peered under my seat. "There's a bomb under you. If you move your weight, it will go off."

"Which one of our suspects knows how to make a bomb?" I gripped the steering wheel, as if by holding on I could save my life.

"Anyone can learn just about anything from the internet." He straightened as a man in bomb gear raced from the building.

He spent a long ten minutes studying the bomb, then shook his head. "How much do you weight, ma'am?"

"One hundred and ten pounds."

"Exactly?"

"How am I supposed to know that? I weigh myself in the morning, naked, before breakfast. I don't know how many ounces." I was going to die. They were going to calculate my weight incorrectly and I'd be blown into a million pieces. I took a deep breath. I wasn't afraid, exactly, but there were still a lot of things I wanted to do before meeting my Maker.

"We'll have to guess," he told Matt. "If we stay within a pound, we should be all right."

"Should be!" I shrieked. "I love you, Matt!"

"Settle down before you blow us all up," the bomb squad guy said. "I'll be back in a few minutes. Don't move."

I didn't plan on it, although my body chose that moment to need the restroom in the worst way. Scared or not, I would not wet myself. I refused. "Is that Wayne in the suit?"

"Yes. He learned about bombs in the army. You're in good hands."

My fingers ached from gripping the steering wheel. I slowly peeled them one-by-one off the leather and exhaled as I settled back in my seat. "I want you to go in the building."

"Not a chance," Matt said. "If you go, I go."

"Roxi needs you. My family will survive."

"Stormi, I'd stay with anyone. The fact that it's the woman I love in danger makes it all the more important. I'm not going anywhere." His look caressed my face.

Tears ran down my cheeks. I'd lied to

myself. I was scared. More scared than I'd ever been. Where was Wayne?

As if my frantic thoughts conjured him, he returned with two sand bags. "I measured these the best I could." His eyes glittered behind his shield. "When I say lift, you lift your rear as high as possible, as fast as you can, so I can slide these in. They're heavy and I don't want to drop them. Do you understand?"

"Better than I've ever understood anything." I positioned my feet against the floorboard of the car in preparation.

"Matt, when I say now, you pull her out. This has to be done in one fluid motion or we're all dead."

Matt nodded, his gaze locked on mine. "Don't die. Angela will kill us."

Wayne chuckled. "I don't plan on it. Ready?" He took a deep breath. "Now!"

I lifted, Matt yanked me over Wayne's back, and Wayne placed the sand bags. The three of us raced for the safety of the building.

The car exploded. The concussion lifted me off my feet and slammed me to the concrete. Glass from the station window rained on my head. But...I was alive.

I rolled over and struggled to catch my breath as my pride and joy, the Mercedes, burned. I could buy a new car. I turned my head to see Matt grinning. I stretched out my hand. "Are you okay?"

"Yes, are you?" He stood and pulled me to my feet.

I nodded. "A bit bruised and got the wind knocked out of me. Wayne?"

"I'm here." He removed his blast shield. "I'm glad you're Matt's girl. Dating you would give me gray hairs."

"You know you love me." Still holding Matt's hand, we limped into the building.

Angela rose from where she'd apparently hid behind her desk and launched herself at Wayne. "I had no idea you were one of those guys. You could have been killed."

"I'm a lot of things, sweetheart, but dead isn't one of them." He patted her head with a gloved hand. "Let me get this gear off and I'll be right back."

I glanced out the shattered window as

a fire truck and ambulance roared into the parking lot. The windows on a nearby squad car were blown out. Still damage to one car and the destruction of another was better than loss of life. My knees weakened and I sagged into the nearest chair.

"Bring her some water," Matt told Angela. "I'll have the paramedics take a look at you. Your head is bleeding."

"So is yours." I moved his hair out of his face.

Two paramedics rushed into the building. One dealt with me, the other with Matt.

Mine shined a flashlight into my eyes. "Possibly a mild concussion, but nothing serious. Does anything else hurt?"

"Just the scrapes on my hands and knees." The fall had torn through my jeans and left my knees bloody.

"I'll clean those up for you. If you want to go to the hospital, you can."

"I'm fine."

"You'll be very sore in the morning." He grinned.

I didn't doubt that for a minute. I

glanced up to see Angela hanging up the phone. "Tell me you did not call Mom."

"Of course, I did. You know how upset she gets when we don't tell her when we're in trouble." She brought me a paper cup of water. "I don't want her yelling at me. I've had enough for one day."

"You've had enough?" I raised my eyebrows.

She shrugged. "Fine, your day is worse. Mom still deserved to know. She said she's going to fix you a hot bath and make soup."

For once, I'd let her treat me like a child. I stood, my body stiffening, and waited for Matt's paramedic to finish doctoring him. He had scrapes, same as me, but nothing that needed hospital care. "I'll drive you home," he said.

"My purse, my gun, and my Tazor were all in the car. I want to replace them before heading home."

"The gun and Tazor, okay, but you'll have to call for your credit cards and driver's license." He took my hand and led me out the back door to his truck.

It suddenly looked very high. The thought of bending my knee enough to climb in caused pain before I moved.

"Let me." Matt scooped me in his arms and deposited me in the passenger seat. With a wink, he moved to the driver's side. "I've been sore before."

So had I, but that didn't mean you'd see me lifting anything anytime soon. I laid my head back against the seat and closed my eyes. We'd been lucky. I smiled. God must still have plans for me, thank goodness. It wasn't time to end my life here on earth.

An hour later, with my body seeming to stiffen with every passing minute, Matt took me home with a new gun, a purple Glock this time, and a new Tazor. He carried me into the house, Mom trotting along beside him, and deposited me on the closed toilet seat. With a kiss and a promise to return later, he left me in Mom's capable hands.

She stared at me, her eyes red-rimmed. "You're going to be a mother. As much as I'll miss the excitement, I think you need to go back to making up stories.

You should have enough fodder by now to write dozens of books."

"You may be right." At least on days like today, I was willing to agree with her.

"A car bomb?" Dakota stuck his head around the door jamb. "Cool."

"It wasn't cool at the time."

"No, probably not. Glad you're still breathing." He ducked back out.

Mom closed the door. "We're creating a family of loony tunes. No one cares about the risks."

Oh, we cared, we just cared about victims receiving justice more. "Where's Roxi?"

"Watching Sesame Street." She turned on the water in the tub. "Strip down while I check on her." She grabbed a packet of Aveeno and sprinkled the flakes into the tub before leaving.

I disrobed and slid into water as hot as I could stand it. As I let the heat soak away some of my aches, I contemplated my next move.

A rental car then a visit to the biker bar. And...I'd hire someone to guard the car while I was inside the bar.

Who would have thought a simple out of town bachelorette party could lead to murder?

20

The next morning, every muscle ached, and I shuffled to the kitchen for a pot of coffee. "'Morning."

Mom chuckled. "With the way you're walking, I guess there isn't anything good about it, except for the fact you're alive."

"Can't say the same about my car."

"Matt dropped off a car for you this morning. The keys are on the foyer table."

Bless that man. "Great. I'd hate to drive that rickety van of yours anywhere." Especially to a biker bar with the words Heavenly Bakes in big cursive letters. There'd be a stampede.

My cell phone rang. Caller ID said it was Pritchard. I exhaled sharply and answered. "Stormi Nelson."

"I haven't heard from you. Is this how you do business?"

"I'm tying up loose ends."

"Her car was blown up!" Mom yelled across the room. "Cut her some slack."

"Excuse me?" Amanda's voice lowered. "Did I hear correctly?"

"Yes. Someone planted a bomb in my car."

"Gracious. Should I be worried?"

"I'm fine, thank you." The selfishness of some people astounded me. "What we've gathered on your case so far is that Dixon took the pictures in an attempt to blackmail you."

"So Lincoln Burnett had nothing to do with it?"

"It doesn't look like he did."

She sighed. "I marched into his office the other day and made a scene."

"I heard. My suggestion to you is to focus on your campaign and leave Lincoln alone. It will only backfire on you if you don't."

"Good idea. Send me the bill." Click. Another name marked off my list. That left Cheryl Miller, Susan Burnett, and the elusive Jordyn Townsend. Not that I thought the officer killed anyone, but I wasn't ruling her out.

I gave Roxi a kiss. "Can you watch her today, Mom?"

"Of course. She loves coming into the bakery. She made her own cookies yesterday." Mom showed me a tray of unidentifiable shapes. "They're delicious."

"Take one." Roxi pointed.

I grabbed a lopsided circle and took a bite. "Yum. Sugar cookie."

"You bit the dog's butt." She covered her mouth with her hand and giggled.

"Did I?" I met Mom's amused glance. "Well, the head is next." I turned the cookie around and took another bite.

"Where are you off to?"

"I'm picking up Maryann and visiting Steak and Leather."

"No one visits that place." Mom frowned. "They get in and out as fast as possible. Alive, preferably."

"I've made friends." I grinned and poured coffee into a travel mug. "If you don't hear from me in an hour, call the cavalry."

Five minutes later, Maryann was sliding into the passenger seat of my rented Mustang and handing me my favorite coffee concoction. "I had Tyler deliver. I think he has a crush on me."

I dumped the plain coffee into the grass. "Thanks. And, any young man under the age of thirty has the hots for you." Her blond curls, blue eyes, and dimpled smile would sway any man, no matter how old.

We parked next to a row of Harleys and I slipped a fifty dollar bill to a man standing outside smoking. He agreed to watch the car for the time it took to smoke a cigarette. I'd take what I could get.

Inside, I squinted through the dim light, spotted Ben Haverson, and made a beeline to his table. "Can I ask you a few questions?"

"Darlin' you can ask me anything." He motioned for us to sit.

"I paid the man outside to watch my car, but I don't have long."

"You have all the time you need." He told someone else to tell the man out front to stay as long as needed. "I heard about the explosion. Scared me for a minute. I thought there wouldn't be any more books. Make sure you put me in one of them stories."

"Guaranteed." I returned his grin. "Did you speak with a police officer by the name of Jordyn Townsend? Dark hair with an attitude?"

"Yeah, she was here. Flashing her badge around like that would make us talk to her."

"What did she want to know?"

"Everything we knew about Dixon, which wasn't much. The man didn't frequent this bar and his daughter skipped town after the funeral. He left her everything, once it clears escrow."

That was nice of him, considering she wanted nothing to do with the man. My heart ached for her, though. She hadn't had the opportunity to make amends, then he'd left her what was probably a lot of money.

"Townsend is missing."

"It happens." He lifted a glass of beer to his lips.

"Come on, Ben. Don't make me dig.

Do you know what happened to her?"

"Can you make your sidekick stop taking notes?" He glowered. "She's making me nervous."

Maryann immediately dropped her pencil.

Ben resumed his talking. "I don't know what happened to her, but she did get into a heated argument with someone in a black SUV in the parking lot. I couldn't see who it was. When they finished their conversation, Townsend got into a navy Chrysler and the SUV sped off."

"You couldn't hear what they were arguing about?" There were a ton of black SUVs in Arkansas. It would be like looking for the proverbial needle in a haystack.

"Nope." He downed the last of the beer in his glass and waved for another. "Don't judge me, sweetie. This is night time for me."

"What do you do for a living, Ben?"

"I work security at the Savings and Loan." He leaned his elbows on the table. "Before you ask, nothing happens there at night. All the action is during the day. That Lincoln Burnett has a parade of angry women in and out from what I've heard."

"Any idea where I should start looking for Townsend?"

"She headed out of here toward the mountain. There are several abandoned camping cabins up there. My guess is…she's hiding out. You still got my number in your phone?"

I nodded.

"Remember. If you get in a tight spot, you call me. Me and the boys will come to the rescue."

"Thank you." I held out my hand, then changed my mind and hugged him instead. "I wouldn't mind an escort to those cabins."

He cleared his throat, his face reddening above his beard. "Me and two of the boys will lead the way." He whistled, pointed out two burly, bearded men, and the group of us trooped out of the building.

I thanked the man guarding my car and once in the Mustang, followed the roar of Harleys up the mountain.

"That was smart asking them to come with us," Maryann said, clicking her seatbelt into place. "I feel tons safer."

"Are you being sarcastic?"

"Yep. They could be luring us to death and rape, and not necessarily in that order."

"I trust Ben. We're safer than we've been since New Orleans."

"Since I trust you, I'll have to accept your judgment."

We turned right onto a poorly graded dirt road, past a sign that read Pleasant Acres Camp site. It wasn't far before I had to stop the Mustang or bottom out.

Ben and one of his guys turned around and stopped next to us. "Hop on, ladies. These hogs can go anywhere."

Maryann didn't look nearly as thrilled as I felt. I wasted no time slinging my purse over my shoulder and climbing on behind Ben. Seconds later, we were bouncing away up the mountain.

Several times, I heard Maryann scream, but since I found it fun, I didn't glance her way. Instead, I kept my eyes peeled for signs of anyone other than us having traveled that way. I tapped Ben on the shoulder.

He stopped.

"Look." I pointed to the side of the road. Booted footprints showed in the loose dirt. "Do those seem new to you?"

"I reckon." He continued on.

Someone had been that way, and I was willing to bet it was Townsend. But, why hide? She was law enforcement. She could go anywhere she wanted to. Unless…she was afraid. She hadn't seemed the type when we'd spoke, but even the toughest person had something they were afraid of. My guess is that Townsend was afraid of dying. Tough exterior or not, I'd caught a glint of uneasiness in her eyes when I'd visited her.

We stopped in a circle of eight rundown log cabins. No one had camped there in a long time, unless you counted kids drinking and smoking pot. A few discarded beer cans and a bong lay scattered next to a ring of rocks.

"The place is quiet," Ben said, sliding

from the bike. "Too quiet."

I agreed. Where birds should have chattered, there was a heavy, eerie silence. I'd experienced it before. The silence of death. "She's here somewhere."

He cut me a sideways glance. "How do you know that?"

"I've experienced this feeling many times. We won't find her alive."

"You're a creepy gal, aren't you?" He motioned for his men to spread out and start searching.

They went one direction, Maryann and I went in the other. I pushed open a rickety door, not expecting to find anything if the layer of dust on the floor was any indication. Still, there might be signs of Townsend having been nearby.

"I am totally freaked out." Maryann grabbed my arm. "No one is in here. We might find a wild animal. Let's move to the next."

"Okay." We jumped from the rickety porch and moved on. Bingo.

This one showed clear footprints. Two sets. One in boots, the other gym shoes with a zig zag pattern on the bottom.

I held up one hand to stop Maryann, and pulled out my gun with the other. I tried to whistle to alert Ben that I'd found something, but all that came out was a whisper and spit. I'd never mastered the art of whistling.

Maryann stuck two fingers in her mouth, blew, and almost shattered my eardrums.

"If anyone was around, they'll know we're here." I glared.

She shrugged. "I'm not going in there."

"Fine. Watch my back."

I pushed open the door and stepped inside. I didn't have to go any further.

Lying in a pool of dried blood next to the fireplace was Jordyn Townsend. She'd been shot multiple times, either because someone was a bad shot or because a battle had ensued.

I turned to examine the doorframe and wall behind me. No bullet holes. The killer had been a bad shot.

"Whoa." Ben came up behind me, clapped a hand over his mouth, and dashed back outside. The sounds of retching drifted through the open window.

I sighed and pulled out my cell phone to call Matt. "I found Townsend. She's dead." I gave him directions to where we were and joined the others outside. I'd learned my lesson about contaminating a crime scene.

I took a seat on the top step and laid my gun next to me. If a trained police officer couldn't find Dixon's killer without getting killed, what made me think I was any better? I hung my hands between my legs and hid behind my curtain of hair.

"Lady, you're as tough as a grizzly bear," Ben said, sitting next to me.

I raised tear-filled eyes.

"I take that back." He patted me awkwardly on the shoulder. "Was she a friend of yours?"

"No, but her death brought up the fact that I'm way over my head with this case. I don't want to die, Ben. I'm getting married next month."

21

"The boys and I will make sure you don't die." Ben gave a definitive nod. "But…we expect wedding invitations."

"Consider yourself invited."

"No, I want a fancy invitation."

I motioned for Maryann to take note. "We'll hand deliver them."

Every time I got involved in a murder, I felt as if I was going to die. How many times could I beat the odds?

To take my mind off the body in the building behind me and how long it would take Matt to arrive, I called the hospital to check on Rusty.

Mrs. Rogers answered the phone. "He's fine. I said I'd take care of him, and I will."

"He means a lot to me. Don't harp because I'm checking on his welfare." I paced the rutted ground in front of the cabin.

"My apologies. Oh, he's waking up." Click.

I guessed he was in good hands. I kicked at a rock, disturbing a pile of pine needles. A ruby earring winked up at me. I'd seen those somewhere before. Using a brown oak leave, I picked up the earring and stuffed it into my pocket.

Sirens wailed in the distance. If the squad cars had the same trouble I did, they'd have a problem getting to the cabins. "Ben, could you and your buddies go give the cops a ride up here?"

He shuddered. "That's asking a lot."

"One of them is my fiancé. Play nice." I watched them roar off on their Harleys, then turned to Maryann who kept glancing at the cabin as if she expected Townsend to come strolling out like a resurrected dead. "Who do you know that wears a ruby earring?"

"Lots of women." She picked up a stick and drew curly Qs in the dirt. "Are you really going to invite Ben and his boys to the wedding? People will shrink back in fear."

"I don't care. They haven't acted wrong toward us, and I count them as friends. Besides," I grinned, "we won't have to worry about any unwanted Paparazzi."

"Like you have a lot of that."

"For a day or two after every murder I solve. Add in a wedding, and flashbulbs are going to be going off."

I stood when the motorcycles came back into view. Behind Ben rode my darling Matt. I sprinted toward him and slammed against him as soon as his feet were on the ground. "Townsend is inside and riddled with bullet holes."

"Are you all right?" He tilted my face to meet his.

"Just grossed out and a bit sad."

He nodded. "Stay here with your…friends." He sighed. "I'll be back out in a few minutes."

"She's safe with us, cop." Ben took a step closer to me.

Matt shook his head, but looked

relieved. Side by side, him and Wayne entered the cabin, leaving Michael to comfort Maryann and keep an eye on us outside.

"Blondie's dating a cop, too?" Ben shrugged. "Danny's going to be sad."

"Which one is Danny?"

"The one looking like he wants to kill that young man." He motioned his head toward a large man that had to weigh close to three hundred pounds. "Don't worry. All he'll do is send dirty looks that way. If these police are your friends, then we'll tolerate them."

"Thank you." I resumed my seat on the top step as a jeep made its way up the road.

Two men jumped out and dragged a fold up gurney from the back. Someone must have warned them that an ambulance would never make it without damage. My question was…where were they going to put the body?

My question was answered shortly. They rolled Townsend out on the gurney, but folded her to put her into the back of the jeep. My mind immediately went to the fact that she had looked very stiff lying next to the fireplace. I couldn't hear, but my imagination filled in the sound of bones breaking. I clapped my hands over them and sang, "La la la la la."

"Lady's lost it," Ben told Matt as he pulled my hands down. "Thinks she's going to die."

"You said that?" Matt's brow furrowed.

"Townsend was a cop and she's dead. Oh. I found this." I handed him the leaf wrapped earring. "I've seen it before, but can't remember right now on whom."

"It'll come to you." He turned to Ben. "Will you take her to her car? Make sure no one tampered with it? I'll ride back in the jeep." He turned and kissed me. "See you at home. Stay there."

I nodded. I'd had enough adventure for one day.

Despite her protests, Michael insisted Maryann ride on the back of Big Dan's bike. Soon, we were bouncing back to the highway and then speeding toward the bar. I grinned at the sight waiting for me.

Harleys circled the Mustang like

covered wagons against Indians. No one was going to touch my rental car. "I owe you big time, Ben."

"Don't forget the wedding invitations. That's payment enough. Oh, and make sure to have lots of good beer. If you don't want to fork out the cash, we'll bring our own."

I laughed. "I'll make sure you're taken care of." I still couldn't help but look under the driver's seat before getting into the car.

"Seriously?" Maryann held her door open. "We find a dead body and you're looking for a bomb? Maybe I should call a cab."

"We're good. I'm just paranoid." I slid into the driver's seat, counted to three, then rolled out as fast as I could, scraping my healing hands on the concrete. "We're good!"

I waved at serious Ben and his friends. They already thought I was losing my mind. What was one more idiotic act?

When we got home, Mom was frosting dozens of cupcakes and setting them on a tray. Smart little Roxi licked off the frosting and put the cupcake back on the other tray. The ones with the unfrosted cakes.

"Uh, Mom? Do you feel as if you'll never finish?" I pointed out what Roxi was doing."

"Oh, for heaven's sake. She's been a wild cat today. You take her for a while." Her eyes narrowed. "Why are your hands bleeding?"

"I, uh, fell out of my car."

"On purpose." Maryann snitched.

Dakota dashed into the kitchen, grabbed two cupcakes, and rushed back out before anyone could say anything. I glanced at Mom, who shrugged.

"What he doesn't know, won't hurt him." She groaned and dumped the cakes into the garbage. "I've been baking all day. I started out at the store, but Roxi acts like she's developed hyperactivity all of a sudden. I think she misses her dad."

"He'll be here for supper." I washed my hands, gently rinsing away the blood, then wrapped them in gauze. "Will you be happy to see daddy?" I knelt in front of Roxi.

"Yes!" She whirled and raced out of the room.

I gave chase as she barged out the front door Dakota had left open. Roxi squealed and chased him down the sidewalk. He glanced over his shoulder and increased his skateboard speed. Grabbing Roxi around the waist, I spun her in a circle. "Let's take Sadie for a walk and burn off some of this energy."

Not the best idea I ever had. Sadie and Roxi both ran circles around me until I lost all control and put the extra leash around Roxi's wrist. At least she couldn't run off. How much frosting had she managed to eat?

Mrs. Olsen watched our progress down the sidewalk, around the cul de sac, then in front of her house before turning off her water hose. "That the detective's kid?"

"Yes." I pulled both dog and child to a halt. "She got into the frosting, and I don't know what Sadie's problem is."

"Lack of discipline." She glanced toward the house and motioned for her husband to stay inside. "Did you notice that SUV is following you?"

"What? No." I turned. Sure enough, there was a vehicle I didn't recognize across the street. "Here. Hold these." I thrust both leashes into her hands and raced for the SUV.

With a squeal of tires, they sped away. Mud conveniently covered the license plate. Townsend might have been killed by someone in a black SUV, now one was cruising my street. My heart skipped a beat as I rushed to get my dog and child and take them home to safety.

"We're back."

Mom shook her head. "Shortest walk in history."

"I think we were being followed." I went around the house checking doors and windows and closing curtains.

Then, I ushered Roxi into the kitchen. "No cupcakes." If I wasn't being paranoid, we needed to stick together. "Should I call Matt?"

"You're really spooked, aren't you?"

"Yeah, but I don't know how much is healthy intuition and what is paranoia after the car bomb and Townsend's death."

"The barista cop is dead?"

"I found her body myself." I put my hands over Roxi's ears. "We shouldn't discuss this in front of her."

Roxi pulled away from me and climbed on a chair to stare out the window. "Go outside."

"Not right now." I sat her on the floor. "Let me get your Legos."

"No." She raced for the living room and yanked the curtains open.

I had no idea how to deal with this behavior. "Roxi, I said no, and I meant it. Settle down or I'll have to put you in the naughty chair." I chose Mom's floral wing chair.

"Not that one. I read to her in that chair." Mom removed a stack of books from a straight back chair we rarely used. "This is uncomfortable. Three minutes here should have her thinking."

I doubted it, but sat her there anyway. "Don't move until I say so or I'm telling Daddy." What a wimp. I couldn't handle a three-year-old. My hands throbbed, my head pounded, and I needed a nap in the worst way. "Want to take a nap?"

"No." Roxi crossed her arms and pouted. "There's a woman looking in the window."

I whirled. Cheryl Miller stared in at us. She smiled and waved.

What now? I couldn't very well pretend we weren't home. "Mom?"

"Yes?"

"Call Matt please and tell him we have a visitor." I held up a finger for Cheryl to wait and moved as slowly as possible to the front door. While I went, I slipped my cell phone into my cleavage. If taken, I doubted Cheryl would look there.

I glanced out the peephole. Dakota stood next to her with a gun pressed to his side.

"Open the door, Stormi, or I'll shoot him. I have no use for a teenage boy. It's the girl I want."

A motherly instinct I didn't know I had welled up in me. I'd do everything in my power to save Roxi. I glanced around the room.

Drat. I'd left my purse in the kitchen, and couldn't very well leave my nephew out there with a maniac.

"Hide and go seek, Roxi." I pasted on a grin and shoved her as far back in the closet under the stairs as possible. "Now hide while Grandma finds you. Shh."

I took a deep breath and opened the front door. "You're making a big mistake."

She shoved past me. "You made the mistake when you butted your nose into my business. Where's the child? I have nothing else in my life and have always wanted a little girl."

I inched toward the kitchen.

"No, you don't. Boy, sit on the sofa. Stormi, you stay in front of me or I'll start shooting. A bullet might ricochet and hit the child where you've hidden her."

I needed to stall Cheryl for the forty-five minutes it would take Matt to arrive. Impossible.

22

"Get the girl or this boy or your mother eats a bullet." Cheryl pointed the gun at Dakota, then at Mom, who stood in the doorway with her cell phone.

Dakota glared at Cheryl from the couch. "I'm not afraid of you."

"You should be." She grinned with all the warmth of a shark. "Everyone in town says I'm crazy. What if they're right?"

"Leave him alone." I glanced around for a weapon, anything I could use to knock the gun from her hand.

"I'm not playing around, Stormi. Get. The. Girl. You can come along if you want, but know that by doing so, you won't live to see the sunset. I surmise that your mother has called the cops.

Whatever. I'll be long gone with my new daughter. Let's go. Now!"

I'd take my chances. Roxi wasn't leaving the house without me.

"Found you." I took my daughter by the hand and led her from the closet. "Let's go for a ride with this lady, okay? We'll get ice cream."

Roxi eyed Cheryl with distrust. "I don't like her."

"You'd better like me," Cheryl said. "I'm your new mommy."

"No." Roxi hugged my leg.

"Get her in the car." Cheryl pointed the gun to the door. "We'll take the Mustang. I'm almost out of gas. Hand me your purse."

"Why?"

"So I can get the keys." She shook her head. "I know you keep a gun in there. I'm not about to let you get it."

Mom chucked my purse at her. It bounced off her head, but other than making her sway a bit, it had no effect.

"Y'all are getting on my nerves." She yanked open the front door. "Unless you want to stay behind with a bullet in the leg, get that child in the car."

I lifted Roxi and followed instructions. Somehow, someway, I'd get help. "Ben Haverson. Steak and Leather," I said.

"What? That doesn't make any sense. We're not going to the bar."

I prayed Mom got the hint as I buckled Roxi into the car seat, pretending to have trouble fitting one end into the other.

"You're driving. Move." She shoved me aside. "I'll buckle her in. Remember…the gun will be pointed at the back of your head. If I have to shoot you, we'll crash."

I climbed behind the wheel with the intention of driving off without her, but the smart maniac climbed over Roxi's seat instead of going around. Maybe she wasn't as crazy as everyone thought.

"Drive east until I tell you to turn."

I did as I was told, passing Susan Burnett who stared with open mouth on the sidewalk. Another crazy woman. At least I'd missed her visit. "You okay, Roxi?"

"Yes, mommy."

"I'm your mommy now, silly dumpling."

I stifled a gag, whether from revulsion or fear, maybe both, at Cheryl's tone. As I drove, exactly five miles over the speed limit per my captor's instructions, I tried to devise a plan that wouldn't get me killed. I didn't think Cheryl would hurt Roxi. Not with her wanting the child as her own. Me…I was expendable.

"Why did you kill Dixon?" I glanced in my rearview mirror.

"He was blackmailing Lance. My love told me that if his wife ever found out about me, he'd break it off." She exhaled sharply. "He did anyway after I killed Dixon. Not that he knew it was me. Oh, no. I'm smarter than that."

"But you were seen kissing Caldwell."

"Aren't you the nosy one? A gal has to make a living, you know. I needed another sugar daddy." She twirled one of Roxi's curls. "My daughter is beautiful. I'm going to teach her that men cannot be trusted."

"They're not all bad."

"Shut up."

I shrugged, figuring we needed a change of subject. "Why Jordyn Townsend? It was you, right? You're missing a ruby earring."

"You found it? I want it back. They were my mother's."

"I gave it to the cops."

She whacked me on the shoulder with the butt of the gun. My right arm went numb. "I should shoot you right now. The earring is precious to me."

"Don't hit me again. If you do, I'll ram this car into the nearest tree and pray Roxi's car seat saves her."

I heard the click of a seatbelt.

"As unsafe as speeding is, I insist you increase our speed. We're being followed."

I'd spotted the black sedan, too, and hoped it was friend rather than foe. I increased our speed another three miles per hour.

"Seriously?" Cheryl hit me again. "You drive like a grandma."

"I can't control the car if you keep

hitting me. My arm is numb."

"Your body is going to be numb if you don't stop playing games. Lose that car."

"Who is it?"

She sighed. "Susan Burnett."

"Why would she be following us?"

"Her and I were talking the other day and I brought up the fact that I would have a daughter soon. She said the same thing. It didn't take a rocket scientist to figure out she planned on taking this little darling here same as me."

"There are two of you wackos wanting my kid?" Maybe I needed to move out of Oak Meadows. It was far from the peaceful town the real estate agent had told me when I bought my house.

"Take the next exit. Do not use your blinker. Wait until the last second to turn." Cheryl barked orders worthy of any Army drill sergeant.

I almost passed the exit, then yanked the wheel to the right. My shoulder screamed in pain. "It didn't work. She's still behind us."

"For crying out loud." She turned in the seat and fired out the back window. "Maybe that will slow her down."

Roxi cried.

"Do not shoot that gun around Roxi!" I slammed on the brakes, jerking us against our seatbelts. "I'll stop right here and let you and Susan fight it out."

"Okay. I agree that was not the wisest course of action for a mother to take. Let's get moving. We're almost there."

We headed into the same part of town I'd almost died at the hands of a gangster girlfriend. Adult bookstores lined the street with liquor stores. Girls in gaudy clothing whistled and waved as we sped by. A group of African American youths gave us dirty looks.

"This car sticks out like a sore thumb," Cheryl said. "Ditch it in that alley. We walk from here."

That was definitely not a good idea. Still, she had the gun, and I didn't.

We piled out of the car and, with Roxi on my left hip, hurried down the alley toward an old apartment complex. Cheryl waved me inside.

"Third floor, second room on the right. This is where I lived before Lance saved me. It's only temporary. I plan on leaving the country in the morning," Cheryl said. "I've already rented a car. I've heard Canada is a beautiful place to live."

The feeling wasn't coming back to my right arm very quickly. If she'd broken one of my bones, I'd throttle her. I didn't want to wear a cast to my wedding.

Cheryl shoved me into an apartment. Peeling wallpaper gave the impression the room had leprosy. I didn't even want to know what had caused the stains on the faded green sofa against the opposite wall. A lopsided dinette with two chairs filled a small kitchen nook.

"I came from very humble beginnings," she said. "Put my daughter at the table. I bought groceries yesterday."

"Ice cream," Roxi mumbled against my neck.

"I don't think the mean lady has any."

"Of course, I do. Strawberry." Cheryl pointed at the mustard yellow fridge in the kitchen. "Go fix her a bowl. What kind of mother doesn't have ice cream in the freezer?"

Crazy ones? Murderous ones? The list was endless.

I served Roxi the ice cream in a paper bowl. At least I didn't need to worry about dirty dishes. I had the horrible feeling that Cheryl has furry company in her squalid abode. I sat in the chair opposite Roxi and folded my hands on the table. I wanted to ask, "Now what?" but was afraid of the answer.

"What to do? What to do?" Cheryl paced the small room. "I'm not sure I want my daughter spending even one night here, but until I can get to the bank to withdraw—" She screamed and pounded the sofa. She called Lance Miller a few choice names I wouldn't repeat, then turned to me. "Call your mother."

"Why?" I frowned.

"Because I don't have any money. You do." She dug in her pocket and pulled out a slip of paper. "Have your mother transfer $100,000 dollars immediately into this account."

I sighed. There went my attic

renovation, any future vacations, etc. I could refuse, but staring down the barrel of a .45 was a great motivator. "Give me your phone."

"Wait. I haven't thought this through." She chewed her thumbnail. "If I give you my cell phone, and you make a call, they'll trace it. They're probably already tracing it." She dropped the phone and hammered it to smithereens with the gun. "There's a landline in the hall. If you keep the call short, yes…that will work. Get up."

She showed me the phone, easily viewable from her doorway. "I will stand here and keep one eye on you and one on my daughter. If you say anything you shouldn't or if you stay on the phone too long, I'll shoot you. Do you want to die here?"

Not really. I shuddered and headed for the phone. Eeew. Who knew what germs were on the thing. I pulled the sleeve of my tee shirt over my hand and lifted the receiver.

Mom answered on the second ring. "Hello?"

"It's me. I need you to transfer money from my account to Cheryl's."

"Thank God, you're alive."

"I can't talk long, or I won't be. Here's the account number."

"You know I'm not going to do that."

"Hopefully, she'll be—"

Cheryl cleared her throat.

"I've got to go. I love you. Tell Matt I love him more than a gangster loves his gardening gal."

"That doesn't make any sense."

"Just tell him." I hung up, hoping he'd decipher the clue.

A few months ago, a killer named Ivy had killed a prostitute with poison ivy from her greenhouse. That greenhouse was only a block from this apartment building. If Matt came, and I saw signs of him being close, I'd find a way to alert him to my location. The cell phone GPS in my cleavage would only get him so close.

"Back inside." Cheryl motioned with the gun.

I wanted to shove that thing right up her rear end. "You're really starting to annoy me with that thing."

"Shut up while I figure out what to do with you. How long does it take for money to transfer?"

"Until morning, most likely. It might be accessible late this afternoon."

"Lucky girl. You might still be alive to see the sunset and rise." She plopped on the sofa, raising a cloud of dust. "So, now we wait."

Unfortunately. Where was Ben Haverson? Or Matt? I honestly thought one or the other would have arrived by now. "Do you have a restroom?"

"Of course I have a restroom. I'm not an animal. First door on your left. Don't even think about trying to escape. There're bars on the window."

I wasn't going anywhere as long as Roxi was here. Pushing open the door, I stepped into a pink bathroom straight from the fifties. I was just plunging my hand into my bra for my phone, when pounding footsteps drew me back to the living room.

Susan Burnett raced into the room. In her right hand, she clutched a revolver.

23

Maybe they'd shoot each other. I moved to stand in front of Roxi. The child had finished her ice cream and stared wide-eyed at the two women facing each other.

"I told you, the girl was mine." Susan planted her feet shoulder-width apart and aimed her gun at Cheryl.

"Keep dreaming." Cheryl's gun pointed at Susan's head. "What we have here is a good old-fashioned western showdown."

One where Roxi and I were trapped in the middle. I glanced at the window next to the table. If I could get it open and shove Roxi out, maybe she could make her way down the fire escape. No, too far. She'd never make it without me, and I didn't think I could get her and me out fast enough.

While the two crazies were trained on each other, I pulled out my cell phone, punched in Matt's number, and set it on the table behind me. If nothing else, Matt would hear what was happening in the room. I eyed the heavy cross necklace. If I could wield the thing—"

"I'm Wyatt Earp," Susan said. "That makes me the winner. Put your gun down."

"Not on your life. I've killed people, you haven't. Adding you to the list isn't going to make me grieve."

My two top suspects. Cheryl had always been my number one. Too bad I hadn't had time to act on finding out who the earring belonged to before getting kidnapped.

Roxi tugged on the back of my shirt. "Daddy is talking."

"Tell him to hush. We don't want him heard," I whispered.

"Be quiet, daddy."

"Help is coming." He quickly said the words I so desperately wanted to hear, then my phone went silent.

In the distance, I heard the wonderful roar of multiple Harleys. Tears sprang to my eyes. Ben had come through for me. He and his boys would have seats of honor at my wedding.

The feeling was returning to my right arm, and I grabbed a nearby broom in one hand and the cross in the other, feeling somewhat like a medieval warrior. While no match for a bullet, if I got close enough, I could deliver a powerful whack to someone's head. Cheryl's head was my first choice.

"You okay, baby?"

"I'm not a baby," Roxi said. She slid from her chair and ran between the gun wielding women. "Play nice." She stomped her foot.

The crazies froze. No doubt, both in fear for their "daughter's" safety. Both eased their fingers off the triggers.

Now was my chance. "Run outside, Roxi!" Holding the broom like a Samurai sword and swinging the necklace, I lunged at Cheryl, bringing the handle of the broom down on her forearm.

She screamed and dropped her gun.

I whirled and swung the cross at Susan's head. She ducked. I swung again, catching her in the knees.

She joined Cheryl on the floor. I was saved by the cross!

I dove for the guns, coming up with one in each hand. "Now, isn't this a wonderful change of events." I grinned.

"It's two against one." Holding her arm close to her side, Cheryl struggled to her feet.

"That's right." I nodded. "Two guns…against none. Sit on the sofa, both of you."

"I can't walk," Susan said. "Why'd you have to hit me? I wasn't going to kill you? I'm not a psycho?"

"You were going to take my daughter."

"You're young enough to have another one."

These two were absolutely clueless. "If you can't walk, crawl."

At that moment, five burly biker men crowded the small apartment. Ben took the guns from me. "You all right, Lady?"

"I'm wonderful now. Where's my daughter?"

"Big Dan has her in the hall. He's good with kids. Do you want me to shoot them?"

"No. There's been enough killing." I rushed into the hall and grabbed Roxi from Dan, holding her tightly to me. "I'll never let anyone hurt you."

"Not as long as we're around," Big Dan said, his voice surprisingly high for such a big man. "You can call me Danny, little one."

She tugged on his beard and giggled.

Still squeezing her tight, I headed down the stairs, knowing Cheryl and Susan weren't going anywhere with Ben and his boys watching them. I stepped into the bright autumn afternoon and sagged to the steps. Now that the danger was over, I let the tears of fear fall. I'd come so close to losing not only my life, but this dear child.

"You know, Roxi. I think I will hang up my PI license and start making up stories again. This isn't the life for a child and I hope to give you a couple of brothers and sisters someday."

"I'm glad to hear it." Matt grinned from a few feet away.

I jumped up and ran to him, squashing Roxi between us. "This was the worst yet."

"Worse than being forced to write a story at gunpoint?"

"Yes."

"Worse than facing down a gang? What about poison octopuses? Or when Cherokee was kidnapped?" He chuckled and wrapped his arms around us.

"Much worse. This one involved our baby."

He rested his chin on the top of my head. "Yes, it did. I've never been more frightened. And, I've been in some tough situations. Thank you for watching out for her."

"I couldn't have done anything else." I lifted my face for his kiss.

He didn't disappoint. He kissed me until everything around us faded and I lost my breath. He kissed me until my knees grew weak and he had to hold Roxi and me to keep us from falling. He kissed me until hoots and hollers brought us back to reality.

I turned to see Ben and the guys marching out the two sullen crazies. I turned away. I had nothing to say to those women.

Three squad cars roared to a stop a few feet from the building while gang members and prostitutes looked on. I slipped my hand into Matt's. "Let's go home."

Together, the three of us made our way to the Mustang. It sat on the road, its tires having been stolen, along with the steering wheel and stereo.

"Hey, Lady!" Ben tossed us the keys to his bike. "Take care of her."

I knew he was talking to Matt and not only about the Harley.

"That's a guarantee." He caught the keys mid-air, then glanced at Roxi. "Now, this is a predicament."

"Those aren't my keys," Ben said, laughing. "Use the bike with the side car."

Matt slung his arm around my shoulders and led the way to our ride.

"Mama."

I turned at Roxi's sweet word. "Yes, baby." I slid my hand into Matt's. "We'll have to make sure she remembers Rachel. She might not have been the nicest person, but she did give birth to your daughter."

He squeezed my hand. "She gave me a great gift, although belatedly, and in the wrong way. Together, we'll make sure Roxi remembers who gave birth to her." He tugged me close and kissed me. "You're kind heart is one of the many things I love about you. Not everyone would care that a spiteful woman such as my ex was gone, leaving a child behind."

I'd lost a parent. Hopefully, the pain I felt at my father's passing would help me comfort Roxi later on.

EPILOGUE

I stood in a rented tent in front of a full length mirror and stared at the woman in front of me. I'd been through a lot in the last year or so, but I'd grown through it all. My faith was strengthened and I was marrying the love of my life. A man who accepted me faults and all.

"You look gorgeous." Mom adjusted my cathedral length veil. "That is the perfect dress for you."

I'd decided to embrace my slenderness. The formfitting dress hugged my arms and upper torso, landing just off the shoulders. The edge of the sleeves fluttered to my wrists. From the knees, the dress billowed out, leaving room to walk and trailed a foot behind me. Swarovski crystals dotted the bodice. I felt like an angel.

Thank you, God...for everything. All that I'd gone through, all that I was, and all that was to come.

Ben Haverson, looking remarkably handsome in a tux, ducked into the tent. "The natives are getting restless."

"I'm ready." I slipped my arm through his elbow. "Thank you for agreeing to give me away. I've never missed my father more than I do at this moment."

"Lady, the pleasure is all mine."

With Cherokee leading the way, followed by Angela, then Maryann and Roxi, we stepped out of the tent onto a white carpet runner. The roar of many Harleys immediately filled the air and I laughed through my tears. "Oh, Ben."

"We wanted you to have a royal send off into matrimony." He grinned through his beard.

When the roar died down, the wedding march began and I took my first step toward my groom.

Matt waited under an arch set up with the lake behind it. The late afternoon rays of the sun sprinkled diamonds on the surface of the water while autumn leaves rained down upon the path in front of me and my guests. It couldn't be a more beautiful wedding.

Ben handed me over to Matt.

I slipped my hand into his, warmed by the tears in his eyes. "I love you."

"I love you," he said, his voice catching. "You are the woman God designed for me."

I smiled through my own tears, not caring if my makeup was mussed.

In a dreamlike state, I heard and did as instructed while the pastor led us in our vows. When it came time to kiss the bride, I didn't wait. I thrust my veil back and wrapped my arms around Matt's neck. He was mine. Officially mine.

Our guests laughed and clapped as he kissed me and dipped me over his arm. All was right in my world.

The End

Dear Reader:

It is with both joy and sorrow that we come to the end of Stormi's gumshoe days. As a wife and mother, it's time for her to leave the dangers behind, except on the page. I hope you've enjoyed the time you've spent with her and her crazy family, and that the love shared between her and hunky Matt made you sigh a time or two.

I have two other cozy mystery series, one beginning with Fudge-Laced Felonies and another with Deadly Neighbors for you to enjoy while I write the first book in a new series, releasing early 2016. I hope you wait impatiently for the Shady Acres stories.

I've enjoyed writing the Nosy Neighbor series, but it's time to move on to something new.

God bless you and keep you,

Cynthia Hickey

Website at www.cynthiahickey.com

A GOOD PARTY CAN KILL YOU

www.cynthiahickey.com

Cynthia Hickey is a multi-published and best-selling author of cozy mysteries and romantic suspense. She has taught writing at many conferences and small writing retreats. She and her husband run the publishing press, Winged Publications. They live in Arizona and Arkansas, becoming snowbirds with three dogs. They have ten grandchildren who keep them busy and tell everyone they know that "Nana is a writer."

    Connect with me on FaceBook Twitter
    Sign up for my newsletter and receive a free short story
    www.cynthiahickey.com

    Follow me on Amazon

CYNTHIA HICKEY

And Bookbub

www.ingramcontent.com/pod-product-compliance
Lightning Source LLC
LaVergne TN
LVHW011808060526
838200LV00053B/3701